Acknowledgment:

I might want to offer my most ρ.υ.υαιια thanks to every individual who has added to the making of this book, "Imperial Sagas". Above all else, I stretch out my genuine thanks to the endless people who have protected and shared the rich history and accounts of the Napoleonic time frame. Their devotion to saving the past has motivated the production of these stories.

I'm obligated to the researchers, students of history, and specialists whose careful exploration and grant have given the establishment whereupon these accounts are assembled. Their experiences and information have enhanced the account and carried profundity to the authentic setting against which these adventures unfurl.

I additionally stretch out my appreciation to my loved ones for their unfaltering help and consolation all through this excursion. Their confidence in me and my work has been a steady wellspring of inspiration and motivation.

To wrap things up, I might want to offer my thanks to the readers who have left this scholarly experience with me. Your interest and enthusiasm for history have powered my own, and it is my earnest expectation that these accounts give you as much pleasure and interest as they have acquired me their creation.

Thank you, from the bottom of my heart.

Nabal Kishore Pande

Disclaimer:

The tales held inside "Imperial Sagas" are works of fiction roused by the verifiable background of the Napoleonic time frame. While large numbers of the occasions, characters, and settings portrayed in these accounts depend on genuinely authentic figures and occasions, artistic freedoms have been taken for the motivation behind narrating.

It means a lot to take note that the author has tried to depict verifiable precision overall quite well; notwithstanding, some creative liberty has been utilized in the retelling of verifiable occasions and the depiction of verifiable figures. Furthermore, certain characters and occasions might have been adorned or adjusted for emotional impact.

Readers are urged to move toward these accounts with a comprehension that they are a mix of reality and fiction and to direct their examination into the verifiable setting encompassing the occasions portrayed. The writer acknowledges no liability regarding any mistakes or misinterpretations that might emerge from the reading of these accounts.

Thank you for your understanding and enjoyment of "Imperial Sagas".

Nabal Kishore Pande

Prelude:

Welcome, dear peruser, to the charming universe of the "Imperial Sagas." Inside these pages, you will leave on an enthralling excursion through the wild time of the Napoleonic time frame, a period of war, unrest, and interest that eternity modified the direction of history.

The Napoleonic period, spreading over from the late eighteenth to the mid-nineteenth hundred years was a period of monstrous change and commotion across Europe and then some. It was an age set apart by the ascent and fall of domains, where rulers conflicted with progressives, and troopers battled for brilliance and distinction on the blood-drenched fields of fight.

Amidst this unrest, Napoleon Bonaparte arose as a transcending figure, a man whose desire and mystique reshaped the political scene of Europe. From his transient ascent to drive as Head of the French to his sensational destruction and exile, Napoleon's story is one of win and misfortune, of success and rout.

Yet, the Napoleonic period was not just around one man; it was an embroidery woven from the existences of innumerable people, each with their fantasies, wants, and fates. From the halls of force in Paris to the combat zones of

Waterloo, the Supreme Adventures annal the existences of the people who considered resisting show and shape the course of history.

Inside these accounts, you will meet a cast of characters as different as the actual period: daring warriors and clever covert operatives, honorable blue-bloods, and brave progressives, all bound together by the strings of destiny and predetermination. Through their victories and afflictions, you will observe the human soul at its strongest and unstoppable, transcending difficulty to accomplish significance notwithstanding outlandish chances.

Yet, the Magnificent Adventures are something other than stories of war and success; they are a festival of human involvement with all its intricacy and magnificence. From the terrific salons of Paris to the rough heaps of Provence, from the clamoring markets of Istanbul to the far-off island of St. Helena, every story offers a brief look into a world loaded with energy, interest, and experience.

As you turn the pages of this book, may you be moved to a general setting where the reverberations of history sound valid, where the deeds of the past proceed to rouse and charm us in the present. May you track down comfort in the victories of the human soul and strength even with difficulty, for in the Supreme

Adventures, the force of narrating is limitless, and the illustrations of history are ageless.

Thus, dear readers, plan to be cleared away on an excursion that would blow anyone's mind, as you dig into the rich embroidery of the Napoleonic time and find the untold accounts of the individuals who hoped for a superior world. For in the pages of the "Imperial Sagas," the previous wakes up, and the soul of experience anticipates those courageous enough to look for it.

The Corsican Conqueror

The sun plunged low not too far off, painting the sky in a stunning embroidery of gold and blood red. Its warm hug encompassed the immense spread of the English Channel, providing a reason to feel ambiguous about the brilliant shine of the uneven waters beneath. On the deck of the great "Bellerophon," Napoleon Bonaparte, Sovereign of the French, remained with a demeanor of calm assurance, his puncturing looks fixed upon the far-off shores of Britain. Close to him, his dearest Josephine, brilliant in the blurring light, radiated a feeling of unflinching help during the twirling flows of vulnerability that lay ahead.

"My dear Josephine," Napoleon's voice extended the delicate lapping of the waves, resounding with a mix of pride and expectation. "We stand on the incline of another period, another triumph."

Josephine went to him, her eyes sparkling with a combination of esteem and concern. "Indeed, my adoration," she answered delicately, her voice a relieving song amid the cadenced orchestra of the ocean. "Yet, let us not fail to remember the imposing test that lies before us. The English are not to be undervalued."

Napoleon gestured, his psyche previously dashing with the essential prospects that lay ahead. "To be sure, my dear," he recognized, his tone certain yet touched with a sprinkle of watchfulness. "Be that as it may, dread not, for we are ready. Our military is considerable, and our determination is steady. Together, we will cut our inheritance upon the chronicles of history."

As the "Bellerophon" cut through the glasslike waters, the unease on board the vessel was overwhelming. Fighters clamored about, their developments deliberate as they made last arrangements for the looming fight, while officials presented in quieted tones, their eyes examining the skyline for any indication of the foe's methodology.

Marshal Ney, Napoleon's unfaltering general, and confided-in comrade, drew nearer with a troubling articulation carved upon his endured highlights. "Your Highness," he saluted cleverly, his voice an orchestra of reliability and assurance. "We are approaching the English coast. Our soldiers stand prepared to do your offering."

Napoleon fastened Ney's arm in a stronghold, a quiet affirmation passing between them. "Much obliged to you, old buddy," he answered, his voice fearless. "Together, we will strike dread into the hearts of our adversaries."

As the "Bellerophon" attracted nearer and nearer to the shores of Britain, Napoleon's contemplations turned internal, reflecting upon the greatness of his desires. He imagined a tremendous realm extending from the sun-kissed shores of France to the far-off land's past, where his standard would be outright and his power unparalleled.

However, during the grandiose levels of his goals, a seed of uncertainty flourished, bothering the edges of his certainty. Consider the possibility that his painstakingly laid plans were to vacillate. Imagine a scenario where his foes ended up being more imposing than expected.

Talleyrand, Napoleon's sharp consultant and expert in strategy, detected the Sovereign's anxiety and moved to console him. "Your Highness," he interposed, his voice smooth as silk yet saturated with an inclination of conviction. "You don't have anything to fear. Our arrangements are careful, and our system is immaculate. Triumph is inside our grip."

Napoleon offered a grave gesture of affirmation, however the heaviness of vulnerability draped weighty upon his shoulders. "I ask that you are correct, Talleyrand," he surrendered, his tone touched with a smidgen of dread. "For the destiny of countries remains in a precarious situation."

In the meantime, on the shores of Britain, Napoleon's looming appearance sent shockwaves resonating through the core of the English foundation. Chiefs of naval operations mixed to reinforce their protections, while legislators participated in intense discussions over the best game plan. In the tumult and disarray, one man arose as an encouraging sign for the English public: Naval commander Horatio Nelson, the unyielding legend of Trafalgar.

From the deck of his lead, the celebrated "Triumph," Nelson reviewed the scene with a steely determination, his sharp eyes missing nothing as they cleared across the turbulent oceans. He comprehended the grave danger presented by the French attack and was ready to do whatever was important to shield the power of his cherished country.

"My compatriots," Nelson's voice blasted across the deck, ordering the consideration of all who remained in his presence. "Today, we face our most prominent test yet. Be that as it may, let us not falter, for we are the children and little girls of Britain, and we will not flounder in that frame of mind of oppression."

The mariners emitted a whirlwind of cheers and praise, their spirits floated by the resolute determination of their regarded chief. With Nelson in charge, they realize that triumph was not simply a goal but rather a certainty, regardless of the expense.

As the days extended into weeks, Napoleon wound up trapped in a maze of strategy and interest, exploring the deceptive waters of worldwide legislative issues with an artfulness brought into the world of need. Gatherings were met with unfamiliar dignitaries, collisions produced and broken in a matter of seconds, as the destiny of countries hung dubiously yet to be determined. Through everything, Josephine stayed an enduring mainstay of help next to Napoleon, her immovable dedication filling in as a wellspring of comfort in the turbulent oceans of vulnerability.

"My dear Josephine," Napoleon commented one night, as they stood together upon the deck of the "Bellerophon," the blurring light of the sunset giving occasion to feel qualms about a warm gleam their countenances. "I could never have requested a more dedicated friend. You are the light that guides me through the most obscure of times."

Josephine grinned carefully, her eyes mirroring the profundity of her love. "Furthermore, you, my affection," she answered delicately, her voice a delicate touch upon the breeze. "You are the stone whereupon I lean. Together, we will face any hardship that comes our direction."

In any case, amid the disorder of battle, there were snapshots of relief, temporary breaks of serenity amid the steady thunder of cannon shoot. On one such event, Napoleon wound up taking part in a confidential discussion with Talleyrand, the two men diving into the complexities of technique and strategies with enthusiasm brought into the world of need.

"Talleyrand," Napoleon's voice was low and pressing, his eyes on fire with a power that gave a false representation of the gravity of their conversation. "Do you accept that we can arise triumphant from this contention?"

Talleyrand respected him with a watchful eye, his face questionable as he gauged his reaction. "Your Highness," he started, his voice estimated and intentional. "Triumph in war is rarely ensured. However, assuming that anybody has the persistence and make plans to defeat the best of obstructions, it is without a doubt you."

Napoleon ingested Talleyrand's words with a combination of appreciation and fear, his brain inundated with the horde of prospects that lay ahead. He knew that the street to win would be laden with danger, yet he stayed immovable in his conviction to see his aspirations understood, regardless of the expense.

Thus, the fight seethed on, each spending day carrying with it a recharged need to keep moving as the restricting powers competed for matchless quality upon the blood-doused fields of war. Napoleon drove his soldiers with a furious assurance, his splendid brain organizing an ensemble of vital moves and determined ploys intended to outsmart his foes every step of the way.

Be that as it may, Chief Naval Officer Nelson, with his unrivaled strategic intuition and relentless purpose, ended up being a considerable enemy, coordinating everything Napoleon might do with an accuracy brought into the world of long periods of maritime skill and resolute steadfastness to his country.

At the unequivocal Skirmish of Waterloo, the two titans of history conflicted in a great battle that would perpetually change the direction of countries. Gun shoot roared across the combat zone, the earth-shaking underneath the heaviness of the steady surge as troopers battled with an intensity brought into the world of distress and assurance.

Riding a horse, Napoleon reviewed the tumult unfurling before him, his heart beating with a combination of expectation and fear. Triumph appeared to be inside his grip, tantalizingly close yet distressingly subtle, as he stressed to perceive the result in the smoke and disarray of the fight.

Yet, destiny, it appeared, had different plans. As the sun plunged beneath the skyline, creating long shaded areas across the blood-splashed fields, a new rush of English fortifications flooded forward, their unfaltering development breaking the floundering purpose of Napoleon's exhausted soldiers.

With crushing sadness, Napoleon looked as his fantasies of triumph disintegrated directly in front of him, his once unassailable realm decreased to nothing yet residue and remains upon the breezes of rout. In that portentous second, he realized that everything was lost.

With crushing sadness, Napoleon gave the request for retreat, his voice conveying across the combat zone like a melancholy mourning for the fallen. His fantasies of magnificence had been run upon the rough shores of the real world, leaving only a heritage stained with the blood of endless lives lost in the quest for his unquenchable hunger for power.

As he rode from the combat zone, Napoleon felt a significant feeling of devastation wash over him, his soul overloaded by the devastating weight of disappointment. However, amid the remnants of his broken dreams, a glimmer of disobedience stayed, shining brilliantly amid the dimness that took steps to consume him.

However Napoleon had been crushed, but his dauntless soul stayed whole, an encouraging sign during the turmoil and hopelessness that immersed his general surroundings. What's more, the same length as there thump of a solitary heart in France, he promised to rise once more, to recover his legitimate spot upon the high position and manufacture another fate for himself as well as his cherished country.

Thus, the adventure of Napoleon Bonaparte, Sovereign of the French, came to a nearby, and his once powerful realm diminished to minimal excess of a reference in the chronicles of history. However, his legend would persevere, a demonstration of the limitless desire and enduring assurance of small time who thought for even a second to challenge the chances and try the impossible.

Eventually, it was not the magnificence of success that characterized Napoleon's heritage, but the unyielding soul of versatility and rebellion that shined brilliantly inside his spirit, moving ages to come to hold onto their fate and shape the course of history in their picture.

The Ballad of Elise

In the core of Paris, where each cobblestone gave testimony regarding the progression of time and murmured stories of former periods, the magnificence of the Dubois domain remained as a getting-through landmark to riches and influence. Its extravagant corridors reverberated with the strides of respectability and the chuckling of revelers, providing a reason to feel ambiguous about a charming spell to all who passed its boundary.

Among the visitors that graced its corridors was Elise, a dream of effortlessness and excellence as she moved with the class of a swan in the sparkling ceiling fixtures and cleaned marble floors. Her brilliant grin enlightened the room as she welcomed every visitor with warmth and appeal, all her developments a demonstration of her childhood as the little girl of Jacques Dubois, a man venerated for his insight and trustworthiness.

"Elise, my dear, you are emphatically brilliant this evening," shouted Madame Dupont, her eyes gleaming with esteem as she moved toward her young companion.

Elise's grin augmented at seeing her dear comrade. "Much obliged to you, dear Madame Dupont. It is a wonderful night, is it not?"

Madame Dupont gestured, her demeanor turning serious as she inclined in nearer. "However, recollect, my dear, in all the charm and party, one must always remember the heaviness of obligation that accompanies our station."

Elise's grin vacillated somewhat as she looked across the space to where her dad, Jacques Dubois, held court with a gathering of recognized visitors. She felt a flood of pride at seeing him, a man whose simple presence deserved admiration and esteem.

"To be sure, Madame Dupont," she answered delicately. "Be that as it may, now and again, the heart yearns for more than obligation and commitment."

Madame Dupont's look mellowed with understanding. "Ok, my dear, love has an approach to making no sense and reason. Yet, proceed cautiously, for the way of adoration is frequently laden with risk."

As though on prompt, a natural figure got Elise's attention from across the room. Henri Leclerc, the dapper youthful official whose very presence set her heart excited, drew closer with a certain step and a beguiling grin.

"Mademoiselle Elise, may I have the pleasure of this dance?" he asked, his voice smooth as silk.

Elise's cheeks flushed with a blushing tint as she acknowledged his outstretched hand. " Monsieur Leclerc. It would be an unparalleled delight for me."

Together, they floated across the assembly hall floor, lost in the inebriating cadence of the music. Their general surroundings blurred into obscurity as they turned and whirled, their giggling blending with the kinds of the ensemble.

However, during the tornado of feelings that moved throughout her, Elise couldn't shake the irritating sensation of disquiet that waited at the rear of her brain. For she realized that their adoration was a taboo one, a fire that shined brilliantly yet took steps to consume them both.

As the night wore on, murmurs of outrage started to course among the visitors, powered by desire and tattle. Jacques Dubois watched from far off, his temple wrinkled with worry as he noticed his dearest little girl laced in the arms of a man whose standing was discolored by murmurs of defiance and distress.

"Elise, my dear, you should be careful," he advised, his voice scarcely discernible over the

25

clamor of the group. "The Leclercs are a pleased and respectable family, yet they are not without their foes."

Elise gestured seriously; her heart weighty with the heaviness of her dad's words. However, attempt as she may, she was unable to control the fire that consumed her, the yearning for an affection that rose above the limits of society and show.

In the meantime, Skipper Antoine, an opponent official whose hatred for Henri Leclerc had no limits, watched from the shadows with an evil glimmer in his eye. His envy powered by a craving for vengeance, he plotted to tear Elise away from the arms of her cherished and guarantee her for his own.

However, during the confusion and unrest that took steps to overwhelm them, there was one consistent presence that offered comfort and direction in the tempest. Madame Dupont, ever the voice of reason in a world gone distraught, remained close by, offering her faithful help and guidance at her breaking point.

"My dear Elise, you should lean on your instinct," she encouraged her voice an encouraging sign in the wild ocean of vulnerability. "For adoration is the main genuine way to joy, regardless of the expense."

Thus, with mental fortitude and assurance, Elise pursued her decision. She overcame the presumption of society and the requests of her station, picking rather to follow the directions of her heart.

Eventually, it was a choice that would characterize her fate. With Henri close by, she fashioned another way, a way enlightened by the radiance of their affection and the commitment to a more splendid tomorrow.

As they stood inseparably, looking out over the roofs of Paris, Elise realized that their process was just barely starting. Eventually, love vanquished all, and nothing could hold up traffic to their satisfaction.

Thus, in the glory of the Dubois bequest, in the murmurs of embarrassment and the reverberations of history, Elise moved to the beat of her heart, her giggling blending with the sound of music as she left on another section in her life, directed by the immortal insight of adoration.

The days passed suddenly of bliss and happiness for Elise and Henri. They took minutes together in the nurseries of the Dubois domain, their giggling blending with the stir of passes on as they said romantic things to one another underneath the shade of antiquated trees.

Yet, as their adoration bloomed, so too did the shadows of interest and misdirection that snuck toward the sides of Parisian culture. Skipper Antoine, consumed by envy and hatred, plotted to destroy them with a shrewdness that had no limits.

One game-changing night, as Elise and Henri took away to the banks of the Seine, their hearts overflowing with adoration and commitment, they were trapped by Antoine and his accomplices. The air popped with pressure as blades were drawn and emotions raged out of control, the moon giving occasion to feel qualms about a shocking sparkle in the scene as the darlings wound up confronting their most prominent test yet.

"Stand to the side, Leclerc," Antoine scoffed, his voice trickling with malignance. "The young lady has a place with me."

Henri's jaw gripped with assurance as he ventured forward, his look enduring. "I won't ever let you lay a hand on her, Antoine. She is mine, presently and for eternity."

Elise's heartbeat was in her chest as she watched the showdown unfold before her. She realized that this was a fight they couldn't win, not against Antoine and his slippery partners.

However, similarly, as all trust appeared to be lost, a figure rose out of the shadows, his presence telling and legitimate. It was Jacques Dubois, Elise's dad, a praiseworthy individual and trustworthiness whose dependability exceeded all logical limitations.

"Enough, Antoine," he blasts, his voice reverberating across the riverbank. "You won't lay a hand on my girl, not while I draw breath."

Antoine's eyes broadened in dismay as he understood that his arrangement had been foiled. With a snarl of dissatisfaction, he and his companions withdrew into the murkiness, passing on Elise and Henri to pause and rest in the consequence of the conflict. Elise's heart dashed with a combination of help and dread, her hands shaking as she stuck to Henri, thankful for her dad's convenient intercession.

"Father, you saved us," she murmured, her voice shaking with feeling.

Jacques embraced his little girl firmly, his eyes loaded up with concern. "I will constantly safeguard you, my dear Elise. No damage will at any point come to pass for you while I draw breath."

Henri gestured thankfully, his look waiting on Jacques with a freshly discovered regard. "Much obliged to you, Monsieur Dubois. You have my timeless appreciation."

With the peril deflected, the threesome advanced back to the security of the Dubois bequest, their hearts weighty with the heaviness of the night's occasions. As they entered the excellent hall, they were welcomed by Madame Dupont, her eyes wide with worry as she took in seeing them.

"What occurred, my dears?" she asked, her voice bound with stress.

Elise described the nerve-racking occasions of the night, her voice shaking with feeling as she discussed Antoine's unfairness and her dad's valiance. Madame Dupont listened eagerly; her temple wrinkled with worry as she handled the weightiness of the circumstance.

"This is alarming for sure," she mumbled, her look glinting between Elise, Henri, and Jacques. "We should proceed cautiously from now on. Antoine won't rest until he has his retribution."

Jacques gestured gravely; his jaw set earnestly. "We will be cautious, Madame Dupont. In any case, we can't permit dread to direct our activities. Love will continuously win eventually."

Thus, with a recharged feeling of direction, Elise, Henri, and Jacques promised to confront anything that difficulties lay ahead with mental fortitude and assurance. They realized that their affection would be tried, yet they additionally knew that as long as they stood together, they could conquer any impediment that held them up.

Days transformed into weeks, and weeks transformed into months as life at the Dubois domain settled once more into a similarity to business as usual. Yet, underneath the surface, pressures stewed as Antoine plotted his best course of action, his hunger for retribution consuming more splendidly as time passed.

In the meantime, Elise and Henri's affection kept on blooming, their bond developing further with each taken second, they shared. They delighted in one another's organization, finding comfort and solace in the information that they were joined in their assurance to conquer anything obstructions held them up.

However, similarly, as they accepted that they had gotten away from Antoine's grip, misfortune hit them with a power that deeply impacted them. At an ungodly hour, a fire tore through the

Dubois bequest, overwhelming everything in its way with a fiery blaze of flares.

Elise and Henri arose to the sound of shouts and the smell of smoke, their hearts beating with dread as they mixed to get away from the consuming destruction of their home. Through the bedlam and disarray, they looked madly for Jacques, their cries muffled by the thunder of the fire.

Yet, they endeavored to no end. As the flares consumed everything in their way, Jacques Dubois was mysteriously gone, his destiny obscure as the hellfire seethed on unrestrained.

In the outcome of the fire, Elise and Henri were left faltering, their reality broken by the deficiency of the one who had been their mainstay of solidarity and direction. Anguish-stricken and devastated, they gripped to one another for help, their adoration the main thing that stayed consistent despite overpowering misfortune.

As they grieved the deficiency of Jacques Dubois, they likewise confronted the terrible truth of Antoine's quarrel, his craftsmanship clear in the annihilation that lay afterward. Yet, regardless of the peril that snuck in the shadows, Elise and Henri would not be cowed, their determination solidified by the memory of Jacques' penance.

Together, they promised to revamp their lives from the cinders of the past, to respect Jacques' memory by living every day without limit and never permitting dread to direct their activities. They realize that their process would be difficult, that difficulties lay ahead that would test their solidarity and versatility to the limit.

In any case, as they stood connected at the hip in the vestiges of the Dubois domain, their spirits solid and their affection consuming more brilliant than at any time in recent memory, they realized that they would confront anything that preliminaries came to their direction with boldness and assurance. For theirs was an affection that had gotten through the fiercest of tempests, an adoration that would endure for the long haul and win over misfortune.

Thus, with heads held high and hearts confident, Elise and Henri left on another section in their lives, directed by the immortal insight of affection and the dauntless soul of flexibility that had united them in any case.

As they looked out over the city of Paris, their eyes land earnestly and their spirits burning with the commitment to a more brilliant tomorrow, they realized that their process was not even close to finished. However, they likewise knew that as long as they had one another, they could defeat any hindrance that held them up and arise more grounded and more joined than at any other time.

For theirs was an adoration that rose above existence, an affection that would persevere forever, an affection that would perpetually shine brilliantly in the obscurity of the world. Also, as they confronted the obscure future that lay ahead, they did as such with unfaltering confidence in the force of affection to vanquish all and the conviction that together, they could defeat anything that hindered them.

Shadows of Espionage

In the complex roads of Paris, where the cobblestones reverberated with the murmurs of shadows, Pierre Lefevre moved with the beauty of a hunter. His presence resembled a wave in the texture of the evening, all his means a quiet statement of dominance over the undercover world he possessed.

"One more peaceful night in the city of lights," mumbled Pierre to himself, his breath shaping a fog in the crisp air. However, in the realm of surveillance, calm evenings were frequently the most perilous.

"Yes, calm without a doubt," came a voice from the obscurity, frightening Pierre immediately before he perceived the recognizable rhythm of Charlotte Dupont, his subtle source.

"Charlotte," Pierre welcomed her with a gesture, his faculties quickly ready. Trust was an uncommon ware in their profession, yet in some way or another, despite everything, he entrusted Charlotte with his life.

"Any report from across the channel?" Charlotte asked, her voice low with a touch of earnestness.

Pierre shook his head, the heaviness of the continuous struggle pushing down on him like a heavy shroud. "Not yet, yet I dread Chief Reynolds is dependably out in front of us."

Their discussion was suddenly hindered by the sound of moving toward strides, reverberating off the tight walls of the rear entryway. Naturally, Pierre went after the handle of his hidden knife, while Charlotte strained alongside him, prepared for anything peril snuck in the shadows.

Yet, shockingly, it was anything but an adversary that rose out of the dimness, yet Colonel Dupuis, the impressive nonentity of French counterintelligence.

"Lefevre, Dupont," he welcomed them with a brief gesture, his eyes sharp as stone. "I trust you are both keeping occupied?"

Pierre constrained a grin, his brain dashing to prepare a conceivable clarification for their presence at an ungodly hour. "Continuously, Colonel. Crafted by a covert operative is rarely finished."

Dupuis respected them with an entering look, as though looking for any touch of duplicity as would be natural for them. Fulfilled, though hesitantly, he slanted his head and vanished once more into the shadows from whence he came.

"Narrow escape," commented Charlotte, her breath turning out in an eased murmur.

"Yes, really close," concurred Pierre, his heart dashing from the experience. In their reality, the line between progress and disappointment was razor-slender, and one wrong maneuver could mean doom.

As they progressed forward with their way, exploring the labyrinth of roads effortlessly, Pierre couldn't resist the opportunity to wonder about the complexities of their reality. Every rear entryway was held confidential, each shadow a possible danger, but, during the confusion, there was a sure wonder to be found.

"The Noblewoman Isabella," pondered Pierre out loud, his contemplations going to the confounding figure who held influence over the courts of Europe with her appeal and sly.

"A perilous lady, certainly," concurred Charlotte, her voice touched with a smidgen of esteem. "Yet, one can't deny her impact."

For sure, the Lady was an awe-inspiring phenomenon — an expert controller who played the round of legislative issues with an expertise that verged on the heavenly. Her coalitions moved like the sands of the desert, her loyalties as whimsical as the breeze, but, some way or another, she generally arose solid.

"Also, what of Commander Reynolds?" questioned Pierre, his brain getting back to their English foe who snuck across the channel.

Charlotte's demeanor obscured at the notice of his name, a demonstration of the firmly established contention that existed between them. "Reynolds is a snake," she spat, her voice thick with hatred. "He will persevere relentlessly to see us fall."

Pierre gestured in a quiet arrangement; his jaw held sincerely. In the realm of reconnaissance, there were no companions, just adversaries masked as partners, and Reynolds was the deadliest of all.

As they adjusted a corner, the overwhelming outline of Notre Woman lingered somewhere far off, its towers coming up towards the sky like quiet sentinels monitoring the city underneath. In the shadow of the church, Pierre and Charlotte stopped, their eyes meeting in quiet comprehension.

"We should be careful," said Pierre, his voice low however unflinching. "For the destiny of countries remains in a critical state, and everything we might do could steer the results for triumph or rout."

Charlotte gestured, her look consistent notwithstanding the vulnerability that lay ahead. "We will win," she promised, her voice ringing with conviction. "For we are the experts of our fate, and no measure of obscurity can douse the radiance of truth."

What's more, with that, they vanished into the evening, two figures bound together by destiny and manufactured in the cauldron of war. In the confounded roads of Paris, where shadows murmured mysteries and the air popped with pressure, their story was simply starting. Also, however, the street ahead was laden with risk, they would deal with it directly, for they were spies — experts of trickiness, gatekeepers of mysteries, and engineers of fate.

The days seeped into weeks, and the weeks into months, yet the round of secret activities indicated that things were not pulling back. Each daybreak carried with it new difficulties, new risks, and new open doors for those able to hold onto them. For Pierre Lefevre and Charlotte Dupont, the dance of trickiness had become natural, their lives a ceaseless pattern of risk and interest.

It was on one such day, as the sun plunged beneath the skyline and the roads of Paris woke up with the sparkle of gas lights, that Pierre ended up entangled in a furtive gathering with an individual specialist.

"Have you heard the most recent?" murmured the specialist, his voice scarcely perceptible over the clamor of the city.

Pierre shook his head, his interest aroused. In their profession, data was cash, and any goody, regardless of how irrelevant, could hold the way to triumph.

"It appears to be the English have caught a shipment of arms destined for Napoleon's powers," uncovered the specialist, his eyes landing with energy. "On the off chance that we don't move quickly, it could mean ruin for our objective."

Pierre's psyche dashed as he handled the data. A shipment of arms could reverse the situation of a fight for Napoleon, and on the off chance that the English had for sure caught it, they would persevere relentlessly to guarantee it never arrived at its objective.

"We should illuminate Colonel Dupuis on the double," pronounced Pierre, his voice critical.

"This could be our opportunity to strike a conclusive blow against the foe."

With a feeling of direction consuming in his chest, Pierre set off towards the central command of French counterintelligence, his brain previously computing the best game plan. Yet, as he explored the clamoring roads of Paris, his contemplations continued to get back to Charlotte Dupont, his always-present friend in the shadows.

It was Charlotte who had first acquainted him with the universe of undercover work, her direction and intelligence molding him into the considerable specialist he had become. Together, they had confronted innumerable risks, impeded various plots, and manufactured a bond that rose above the turmoil of war.

As he moved toward the central command, Pierre's contemplations were interfered with by seeing Colonel Dupuis remaining at the entry, his harsh appearance enlightened by the glimmering light of the gas lights.

"Lefevre," welcomed Dupuis, his voice blunts however not harsh. "What brings you here at this hour?"

Pierre burned through no time in transferring the data he had accepted, his words tumbling out in a hurry of earnestness. "The English have caught a shipment of arms implied for Napoleon's powers," Pierre made sense of, his breath coming in short erupts from the scramble of his excursion. "We really must demonstrate quickly to keep this from influencing the overall influence in support of themselves."

Colonel Dupuis listened eagerly; his foreheads wrinkled at the profound idea. "This is disturbing news without a doubt," he yielded, his tone grave. "We can't permit the foe to acquire such a critical benefit."

Pierre gestured in understanding, his psyche previously hustling with possible systems to frustrate the English capture attempt. "With your consent, Colonel, I will gather a group and devise an arrangement to recuperate the arms before it's past the point of no return."

Dupuis respected Pierre with a deliberate look, his demeanor unintelligible. "Great, Lefevre. You have my approval. However, recollect, disappointment isn't a choice. The destiny of our country lies on your shoulders."

With a fresh salute, Pierre changed direction suddenly and rushed into the base camp, his considerations consumed by the errand ahead. He realized the dangers implied in such a mission — the chance of catch, of treachery, of death — however, he likewise realized that the stakes were too high to even consider disregarding.

Inside, he found Charlotte sitting tight for him, her eyes landing with expectation. "What did Dupuis say?" she asked, her voice scarcely over a murmur.

Pierre handed off the subtleties of their discussion, his words interspersed by a need to keep moving. "We want to move rapidly," he demanded, his look locking with Charlotte's. "Accumulate our most confided-in agents. We leave at first light."

Charlotte gestured in a quiet arrangement, her determination reflecting his own. Together, they set about collecting their group — a ragtag gathering of spies and saboteurs, each handpicked for their one-of-a-kind abilities and faithful reliability.

As the primary light of daybreak crawled over the housetops of Paris, Pierre and his group accumulated external the base camp, their breath framing mists in the crisp morning air. They were wearing dull clothing, their countenances clouded by veils and hoods, prepared to vanish into the shadows immediately.

"We have something important to take care of," pronounced Pierre, his voice consistent notwithstanding the gravity of their main goal. "The destiny of our country remains in a critical state, and it depends on us to guarantee that the arms arrive at Napoleon's powers unblemished."

With a quiet gesture, the group set off into the core of the city, their strides reverberating off the cobblestones as they advanced toward the meeting point. En route, they experienced watches of English fighters, their presence a consistent sign of the perils that prowled in the shadows.

However, Pierre and his group were not stopped. With every hindrance they experienced, they figured out how to beat it, whether through covertness, trick, or sheer power of will. They moved like phantoms through the roads of Paris, their developments were liquid and exact, their faculties sharpened to a razor's edge.

At last, they arrived at the edges of the city, where the arms shipment was supposed to be covered up. As they crawled through the underbrush, they detected the obvious glimmer of metal somewhere far off — an escort of English fighters protecting their award.

Pierre reviewed the scene with a basic eye, his brain previously devising a game plan of assault. "We'll part into two gatherings," he murmured to Charlotte and the others. "One will make a redirection to draw the fighters away, while the other will move in to get the arms."

With rehearsed accuracy, the group got a move on. Charlotte and a modest bunch of agents set off towards the guard, their developments quick and quiet, while Pierre and the rest situated themselves for the trap.

As the principal shots rang out, disorder emitted in the clearing. English troopers mixed for cover, their yells muffled by the snap of gunfire. Amidst the disarray, Pierre and his group moved in with dangerous productivity, dispatching their enemies with a progression of fast, definitive strikes.

However, similarly, as they were going to get the arms, a natural voice sliced through the bedlam — a voice that sent a chill down Pierre's spine.

"Heading off to some place, Lefevre?"

It was Skipper Reynolds, flanked by a crew of his best men, their rifles prepared in Pierre and his group. His face was a cover of conceited fulfillment, his eyes sparkling with win.

Pierre's heart sank as he understood they had been driven into a snare. However, there was no time for lament, no space for uncertainty. With a quiet sign, he and his group got a move on, the foe in a savage fight for control of the arms.

The air was thick with the sound of gunfire, the harsh smell of explosives hanging weighty in the air. Pierre battled with a fierceness brought into the world of urgency, all his developments a dance of death and obliteration.

Yet, regardless of their earnest attempts, the chances were against them. Reynolds and his men battled with a tenacious assurance, their prevalent numbers gradually acquiring the high ground.

Right when everything appeared to be lost, an unexpected blast shook the clearing, sending garbage flying this way and that. Through the smoke and residue, Pierre got a brief look at Charlotte and different agents, their countenances not entirely settled.

"Go!" yelled Charlotte, her voice scarcely perceptible over the racket of the fight. "We'll hold them off!"

With a gesture of much obliged, Pierre jumped all over the chance and made a run for it, the arms gripped firmly in his grip. Behind him, he could hear the hints of gunfire and yells of rebellion as Charlotte and the others hung tight against overpowering chances.

As he vanished into the security of the encompassing woods, Pierre saved a second to look back at the location of the fight. Through the dimness of smoke and tumult, he could see Charlotte standing tall during the slaughter, her edge blazing in the daylight as she battled close by her confidants.

With overwhelming sadness, Pierre dismissed and vanished into the shadows, realizing that their penance wouldn't be neglected. For in the realm of reconnaissance, where risk prowled everywhere and double-crossing was a dependable friend, it was the obligations of fellowship and reliability that genuinely made a difference.

Furthermore, as he vanished into the wellbeing of the backwoods, Pierre promised to respect those bonds with each breath he took, for they were the genuine cash of the secret world he possessed — a reality where the line between companion and enemy obscured as time passes, and simply the valiant thought for even a moment to step.

The Dueling Musketeers

In the sun-soaked fields of Gascony, where the murmuring breeze conveyed stories of courage and honor, two figures moved with an elegance that appeared to be practically powerful. Alexandre Dumas and Gaston Duval, their names inseparable from courage and fellowship, competed underneath the purplish-blue sky, their swords blazing like lightning against the verdant setting.

"Watch your balance, Gaston," Alexandre called out, his voice loaded up with the simple commonality of a long-lasting companionship. "You leave yourself excessively open."

Gaston laughed, his eyes landing with gaiety. "Ok, yet you neglect, my dear Alexandre, I have a couple of stunts at my disposal yet."

Their chat reverberated through the preparation grounds, a song of chuckling and steel that appeared to resound for a significant distance around. Yet, in the happiness, there waited an implicit figuring out between the two men - a bond produced in the pot of fight, where life and passing moved connected at the hip.

As they orbited one another, their developments liquid and exact, the tranquility of their reality was broken by the appearance of another figure. Colonel Rochefort, his uniform flawless and his stance inflexible with power stepped into the post like a tempest cloud not too far off.

Gaston glared, his look glinting at Alexandre. "Who is that, Alexandre? I don't remember him."

Alexandre's appearance was obscured as he watched the novice approach. "That, old buddy, is Colonel Rochefort. I have heard murmurs of his standing - not a solitary one of them good."

Without a doubt, Colonel Rochefort radiated a demeanor of haughtiness that appeared to separate him from the men around him. His eyes, sharp as stone, overviewed the preparation grounds with a derisive scoff, as though he found the actual sight of Alexandre and Gaston underneath him.

Gaston shuddered, his hand fixing around the grip of his blade. "He conducts himself as though he were destined to order. However, mark my words, Alexandre, there is inconvenience blending."

Alexandre gestured; his jaw set earnestly. "We will watch out for him, Gaston. Something lets me know he isn't reliable."

Their doubts were before long affirmed when Colonel Rochefort made his goals understood.

With a haughty throw of his head, he gave a test to Alexandre, his voice bound with not at all subtle hatred.

"I see you extravagant yourself a fighter, Dumas," Colonel Rochefort scoffed. "Be that as it may, can you back up your brags with steel?"

Alexandre's look was limited, his hand floating naturally as far as possible of his sword. "I acknowledge your demand, Rochefort. Yet, know this - I battle not so much for greatness or pride, but rather for honor."

The stage was set for a standoff that would reverberate through the records of history. As the sun plunged underneath the skyline, creating long shaded areas across the dueling ground, the air popped with strain.

Marianne Leclerc, the vivacious proprietor of the close by bar, observed as a passive spectator, her heart conflicted between the two men who held her kind gestures. She had known Alexandre since they were kids, their bond produced through shared chuckling and murmured confidences.

"Alexandre," she murmured, her voice scarcely discernible over the mumbles of the group. "Kindly, watch out."

Yet, Alexandre just grinned, his eyes meeting hers with a consoling warmth. "Dread not, my dear Marianne. I will arise successfully, for yourself and for every one of the people who have confidence in me."

With a twist, Alexandre drew his sword, the steel glimmering in the blurring light. Across the dueling ground, Colonel Rochefort reflected on his developments, his demeanor one of cold assurance.

The conflict of steel broke the quiet, sending shockwaves through the collected group. With each attack and counter-attack, Alexandre and Rochefort moved a lethal three-step dance, their developments a haze of speed and accuracy.

"Is that everything you can manage, Dumas?" Colonel Rochefort provoked, his voice conveying across the front line.

In any case, Alexandre stayed relentless, his center enduring as he searched out the shortcomings in his adversary's safeguard. With a quick bluff, he allowed Colonel Rochefort to stay uncovered, his edge tracking down its imprint with dangerous precision.

The group emitted cheers as Colonel Rochefort staggered in reverse, his sword tumbling from nerveless fingers. With a victorious yell,

Alexandre raised his edge high, an encouraging sign in the social occasion obscurity.

In any case, during the confusion, Marianne's heart was weighty with struggle. She had consistently realized that her affections for Alexandre ran profound, however presently, as she watched him loll in the reverence of the group, she understood the profundity of her adoration for him.

"Alexandre," she mumbled, her voice shuddering with feeling. "I can't deny reality any longer. I love you."

Also, as Alexandre went to confront her, his eyes sparkling with triumph, Marianne realized that their process was nowhere near finished. Together, they would confront anything that difficulties lay ahead, their affection a directing light in the haziness of vulnerability.

For in the core of Gascony, during the conflict of steel and the thunder of the group, Alexandre Dumas and Marianne Leclerc had tracked down their predetermination. Also, nothing, not even the progression of time, could diminish the fire that consumed them.

As the days transformed into weeks and the weeks into months, Alexandre and Marianne's adoration bloomed like a blossom in the springtime. They strolled connected at the hip through the fields of Gascony, their chuckling blending with the stir of the breeze in the trees.

Be that as it may, their recently discovered joy was destined to be tried by powers outside of their reach. Colonel Rochefort, nursing his injured pride, plotted his vengeance in the shadows, his contempt for Alexandre putrefying like an injury.

"I won't rest until I have seen Dumas pushed to the brink of collapse," Colonel Rochefort promised, his voice low and venomous. "He might have won the fight, however, the conflict is not even close to finished."

In the meantime, Gaston Duval, ever faithful to his companion, watched with developing worry as Alexandre's relationship with Marianne extended. He had long held onto affections for the energetic bar proprietor, his heart hurting with implicit craving.

"Alexandre," Gaston wandered one night, as they sat underneath the stars with the aroma of wildflowers in the air. "I should talk with you about Marianne."

Alexandre went to his companion, his temple wrinkled with disarray. "What is it, Gaston? Has something occurred?"

Gaston wavered, his look glinting to the ground. "It's an obvious fact that I care for Marianne profoundly, Alexandre. Yet, I dread that my sentiments might be making me act unreasonably."

Alexandre's heart held with understanding. "Gaston, old buddy, you want not stress. Marianne and I are appreciative of your fellowship; however, our affection is valid and unshakeable."

Gaston gestured, a weak grin playing at the edges of his lips. "I know, Alexandre. What's more, I truly do never really divide you and Marianne. In any case, guarantee me this - guarantee me that you will continuously love her, for she is an uncommon fortune for sure."

"I guarantee," Alexandre promised, his voice touched with feeling. "I will cherish her until my perishing breath."

Thus, during the unrest of their lives, Alexandre and Marianne gripped one another with a furious assurance. They realize that the street ahead would be difficult, however, with the length of they had one another, they could endure any hardship that came their direction.

In any case, much to their dismay their most noteworthy test lay just into the great beyond, prowling in the shadows like a hunter standing by to strike. Colonel Rochefort, consumed by his hunger for retribution, had focused on obliterating all that Alexandre held dear.

As the days extended into weeks and the weeks into months, Colonel Rochefort's plans developed always intricate, his disdain for Alexandre pushing him to the edge of frenzy. He would persevere relentlessly to see his adversary brought low, regardless of whether it implied forfeiting all that he held dear.

In the meantime, Alexandre and Marianne delighted in the straightforward delights of their coexistence, their adoration developing further as time passed. They moved underneath the stars and murmured mysteries in the murkiness, their hearts entwined like the parts of a contorted oak tree.

However, as murmurs of Colonel Rochefort's unfairness started to spread through the open country, Alexandre realized that they couldn't stand to let down their watchman. Peril prowled everywhere, standing by to jump out of the blue.

"We should be watchful, Marianne," Alexandre asked his voice grave with concern. "Colonel Rochefort will persevere relentlessly to see me annihilated, and I dread that you might be in peril also."

Marianne gestured, her eyes sparkling sincerely. "I won't allow dread to control my life, Alexandre. We have confronted many difficulties together, and we will confront this one too."

Thus, with hearts brimming with mental fortitude and assurance, Alexandre and Marianne arranged to stand up to the approaching danger that loomed over their heads like a foreboding shadow. They realize that the street ahead would be laden with hazard, however as long as they had one another, they were prepared to confront whatever lay available.

In any case, much to their dismay their most noteworthy test was on the way, an intense test time that would stretch them to the actual edges of their solidarity and strength. Colonel Rochefort, consumed by his hunger for retaliation, had released a power that even he had no control over - a power that took steps to destroy their reality at the creases.

As the last confrontation moved close, Alexandre and Marianne stood next to each other, their hands caught tight in a quiet promise of fortitude. They realize that the situation is anything but favorable for them, yet they wouldn't withdraw in that frame of mind of difficulty.

"We will confront this together, Alexandre," Marianne murmured, her voice shaking with feeling. "Regardless, we will confront it together."

What's more, with that promise ringing in their ears, they walked forward to meet their fate, their hearts on fire with the searing energy of genuine affection. For in the core of Gascony, during the conflict of steel and the thunder of the group, Alexandre Dumas and Marianne Leclerc had tracked down their predetermination, yet in addition, the solidarity to manufacture their way even with difficulty. Also, as long as they had one another, they realized that they could beat any obstruction that held them up.

A Waltz with Destiny

In the brilliant assembly halls of Vienna, where plushness dribbled from each crystal fixture and each aristocrat and woman skimmed across the marble floors with rehearsed tastefulness, Marie Lefevre remained as a signal of elegance and refinement. Her childhood as the little girl of a French negotiator had blessed her with a demeanor of refinement that was unequaled, her magnificence a murmured legend among the gentry.

As the ensemble played and the artists twirled around her, Marie's brain meandered. Notwithstanding the stunning environmental factors, she felt a feeling of dissatisfaction sneaking in. The lavishness and triviality of elegant life appeared to choke out her soul, leaving her longing for something more profound, something more significant.

"You look decidedly brilliant this evening, Marie," a voice interfered with her viewpoints. It was Louis Durand, a beguiling blue blood whose presence never neglected to give her a much-needed boost.

Marie grinned considerately, however, her psyche was somewhere else. "Much obliged to you, Louis. The ball is without a doubt charming."

Louis laughed, his blue eyes shimmering with naughtiness. "Ok, however not so charming as you, my dear Marie. Will we dance?"

Before Marie could answer, a tall figure moved toward them, his presence telling consideration. It was Count Philippe, a strange aristocrat whose standing went before him.

"Mademoiselle Lefevre," Count Philippe welcomed her with a slight bow. "May I have the pleasure of this dance?"

Marie's heart skirted a thump as she met his serious look. There was an attractive thing about Count Philippe, something that attracted her to him like a moth drawn to.

" Count Philippe," she answered, unfit to oppose his appeal.

As they took to the dance floor, Marie ended up dazzled by Count Philippe's easy effortlessness. They moved fitting together beautifully, the music twirling around them like a tornado of feeling.

"I should say, Marie, you have a remarkable ability for moving," Count Philippe commented, his voice low and smooth.

Marie giggled, experiencing a glow spread through her veins. "Furthermore, you, Count Philippe, are a remarkable artist yourself."

Their discussion streamed effectively as they moved, addressing everything from governmental issues to verse. Marie was captivated by Count Philippe's energy for equity and correspondence, and his intense confidence in the force of individuals to achieve change.

Yet, amid the chuckling and the music, Marie couldn't shake the sensation of contention fermenting inside her. Louis addressed all that she had at any point known - steadiness, solace, and security. However, Count Philippe offered her something limitlessly really tempting - the opportunity to be important for an option that could be more significant than herself, to battle for the privileges of the mistreated and oppressed.

As the night wore on, Marie wound up conflicted between her dependability on Louis and her expanding affection for Count Philippe. It was a fight pursued in her heart as well as in the turbulent scene of progressive Europe.

The undeniable trends were clearing across the mainland, causing turmoil and discontent among the majority. Wherever Marie looked, she saw the indications of upset - the murmurs of dispute, the thunderings of resistance.

Trapped in the crossfire of history, Marie realized that she was unable to stay uninvolved any longer. She needed to settle on a decision, a decision that would decide the course of her life and the destiny of her country.

Thus, with crushing sadness and a steely determination, Marie settled on her choice. She would follow Count Philippe into the core of the unrest, neglecting the wellbeing of her special childhood for the commitment of a more promising time to come for all.

As she remained on the edge of another time, Marie felt a flood of trust and assurance. The way forward would be full of risk and vulnerability, however, she would walk it with her head held high, realizing that she had picked the most genuine way of all - the way of opportunity, uniformity, and equity for all.

Days transformed into weeks, and weeks transformed into months as Marie hurled herself entirely into the reason with unflinching commitment. Along with Count Philippe and their kindred progressives, she traversed Europe, mobilizing support for their honorable undertaking.

Their process was not without its difficulties. They confronted resistance every step of the way, from the people who stuck obstinately to the old request to the individuals who tried to take advantage of the disarray for their benefit. Yet, Marie would not be hindered, drawing strength from the uprightness of their objective and the fellowship of her confidants.

En route, she experienced people whose accounts contacted her profoundly - people from varying backgrounds who had been squashed underneath the impact point of mistreatment. Their experiences energized her assurance, helping her to remember the criticalness of their central goal and the lives that remained in a precarious situation.

As Marie dove further into the core of the upset, she ended up confronting tough decisions and inconceivable penances. There were minutes when uncertainty sneaked in when the monstrosity of their undertaking took steps to overpower her.

However, each time she vacillated, Count Philippe was there to consistent her, his unfaltering faith in her wouldn't ever falter. Together, they continued onward, their bond developing further as time passed.

And afterward, when triumph appeared to be inside their grip, misfortune struck. Amidst a wild fight, Count Philippe fell, his life doused in a blast of greatness.

For Marie, it was an overwhelming blow, one that shook her profoundly. In the outcome of his demise, she thought of herself as loose, wrestling with pain and depression.

Be that as it may, even at her breaking point, Marie wouldn't leave the reason for which Count Philippe had given his life. With restored assurance, still up in the air to respect his memory and satisfy their common long for a superior world.

Eventually, it was not the charm of sentiment or the solaces of honor that influenced Marie's choice, but rather the savage conviction of her own heart. With immovable determination, she decided to proceed with the battle, realizing that the penances they had made were not to no end.

As the residue settled and the air cleared, Marie rose out of the pot of insurgency, a changed lady. However the scars of the fight would constantly remain, they filled in as a sign of the cost of opportunity and the unyielding soul of the people who battled for it.

Also, however, Count Philippe was gone, his heritage lived on in the hearts of all who had known him. His penance could never be neglected, and his vision of a more pleasant, all the more society was an encouraging sign for a long time into the future.

Concerning Marie, she kept on strolling the way they had manufactured together, her soul whole and her purpose immovable. Eventually, she realized that genuine opportunity was not won on the front line, but rather in the hearts and brains of the people who hoped for a superior world.

Marie's process was not without its hardships, but rather through everything, she stayed unfaltering in her obligation to the reason. En route, she experienced numerous who shared her vision for a more promising time to come, everyone adding their voice to the chorale of progress.

Together, they worked resolutely to destroy the harsh frameworks that had long held influence over their lives, confronting misfortune with mental fortitude and assurance. Furthermore, however, the street ahead was full of risk, and Marie realized that she was unable to flounder, not when so a lot was in question.

As the upheaval picked up speed, Marie wound up pushed into an influential position, directing her friends with shrewdness and empathy. It was an overwhelming liability, yet one she embraced earnestly, realizing that the destiny of endless lives rested in her grasp.

Also, as she stood at the front of the battle, Marie understood that she was in good company. Behind her stood an army of courageous people, joined as they continued looking for opportunity and equity. Theirs was a battle for themselves, yet for people in the future yet unborn, a battle that would shape the course of history for quite a long time into the future.

Eventually, Marie's penances were not to no end. The upheaval succeeded, introducing another time of illumination and progress. Furthermore, however, the street ahead would without a doubt be troublesome, Marie confronted it with trust in her heart, realizing that what was to come held unlimited opportunities for those able to battle for what they had confidence in.

As she glanced out over the recently freed city, Marie felt a feeling of satisfaction expand inside her. The battle had been long and laborious; however, it had been worth the effort, each penance, each difficulty, each tear shed for the sake of opportunity.

Also, as she remained there, encompassed by the happy cheers of her kindred progressives, Marie realized that she had at last tracked down her actual calling. She was at this point not simply Marie Lefevre, a little girl of a French representative, but Marie Lefevre, a hero of individuals, an encouraging sign in a world over and over again covered in haziness.

For Marie, the transformation was a part of ever, however, the vital crossroads of her life, a demonstration of the force of boldness, assurance, and the strong human soul. Furthermore, however, her process was not even close to finished, she confronted the future with a recharged feeling of direction, knowing that for however long there were treacheries to be corrected and opportunities to be won, she would continuously be prepared to answer the invitation to battle.

The Art of War

In the rugged breadth of the Provence mountains, where the noise of contention reverberated through the valleys and bluffs, Chief Jean-Luc drove his band of guerrilla contenders with an enthusiasm as extreme as the noontime sun pounding upon them. His endured face bore the characteristics of insubordination, each scar portraying a story of opposition against the infringing powers of Napoleon, who looked for territory over their country.

Standing side by side with him was Anaëlle Moreau, a lady whose unyielding soul consumed as furiously as the open air fire on a cold evening. With her rifle fastened in a delicate hug, she moved with the ease of an artist and the accuracy of a carefully prepared sharpshooter. Her sky-blue eyes, mirroring the unending territory of the cloudless sky, held onto a relentless purpose to free her kin from the grip of persecution.

Their association was manufactured in the cauldron of difficulty, each snapshot of brotherhood and shared hazard restricting them closer together. As they explored the unsafe territory, each step a quiet statement of their opposition, Jean-Luc and Anaëlle shared an association that rose above the disorder of fight.

"One more day, another conflict," Jean-Luc commented, his voice resounding off the gorge walls like far-off thunder. "In any case, we should stay careful. The adversary is tricky, and they will persevere relentlessly to pulverize our rebellion."

Anaëlle gestured, her look fixed on the far-off skyline where the French powers lay on pause. "We can't stand to vacillate now," she answered, her voice relentless notwithstanding the adrenaline flowing through her veins. "Our kin seek us for authority, for trust."

Their discussions, frequently murmured underneath the shroud of night, overflowed with criticalness and assurance. They planned, arranged their best courses of action, and reinforced each other's spirits with uplifting statements and fortitude.

Yet, during the disturbance of battle, there was a flash between them. A common look, a transitory touch, said a lot without the requirement for words. What's more, as they battled next to each other, their bond extended, entwined with the actual texture of their reality.

"It's something beyond endurance now, Anaëlle," Jean-Luc admitted one night as they sat by the popping fire, its glow a consoling differentiation to the chill of the evening. "It's tied in with producing a future worth living. A future where our youngsters can inhale free."

Anaëlle went after his hand, her touch establishing him in the mayhem encompassing them. "I trust in that future, Jean-Luc," she said delicately, her voice a delicate breeze in the tempest. "What's more, I put stock in us. Together, we can defeat any snag."

Their second was broken by the unexpected ejection of gunfire somewhere far off, the sharp reports slicing during that time like a sickle through wheat. With a common look, Jean-Luc and Anaëlle got a move on, resolve immovable notwithstanding the risk.

The appearance of Colonel von Heinz, an unfeeling foe known for his ruthlessness, increased the stakes of their battle. His presence cast a pall of dread over their positions, each move determined to pulverize their opposition.

"We can't fall before von Heinz and his sidekicks," Jean-Luc declared, his voice conveying across the camp. "We should stand firm, joined in our assurance to own this."

Anaëlle gestured, her eyes blazing with resistance. "For each foul play they incur, we will dispense equity," she pronounced, her words an energizing sob for their goal. "They might have the numbers, yet we have something they come up short on strength of our convictions."

Thus, they battled on. With each snare and strike, they struck dread into the hearts of their foes, their activities a demonstration of their expertise and crafty. However, in the bedlam, during the slaughter and agony, there was trust.

In the rough piles of Provence, in the whirlwind of the fight, Commander Jean-Luc and Anaëlle Moreau remained as reference points of versatility, their affection a directing light in the haziness. Furthermore, however, their process was laden with danger, they knew that together, they were invulnerable.

As days transformed into many weeks into months, their guerrilla strategies became bolder. They assaulted supply lines, attacked stations, and trapped adversary watches with savage proficiency. Every triumph supported their purpose, energizing their assurance to challenge Napoleon's oppression.

Yet, with each win came an expense. They covered confidants, companions, friends, and family, their penances a bleak sign of the cost of opportunity. However, even notwithstanding misfortune, Jean-Luc and Anaëlle wouldn't yield. Their bond was fortified with every difficulty, mooring them in the tumult of war.

One twilight evening, as they rested underneath an overhang of stars, Jean-Luc shared stories of his young life — a period before the conflict, when the mountains reverberated with giggling instead of gunfire. Anaëlle listened eagerly, her heart weighty with yearning for the harmony they once knew.

"I long for a day when the mountains will be quiet in the future," she admitted, her voice scarcely over a murmur. "At the point when our kids can play without dread, and our kin can live without abuse."

Jean-Luc caught her hand in his, his touch a consolation in the haziness. "That day will come, Anaëlle," he promised, his voice touched with conviction. "We will battle until every French warrior has withdrawn from our properties."

Their determination was tried consistently. They confronted ambushes, double-crossings, and close to brushes with death. Be that as it may, through everything, they stayed relentless, drawing strength from one another as they walked ever ahead.

Then, on a pivotal day in the intensity of summer, they got an expression of an unequivocal fight — an opportunity to strike a devastating blow against Napoleon's powers. Jean-Luc and Anaëlle mobilized their warriors, their spirits burning with the possibility of triumph.

As they surged into a fight, the conflict of steel and the roar of cannon fire consumed the space. Jean-Luc drove from the front, his voice ringing out over the disorder, while Anaëlle took out aggressors with dangerous exactness.

For quite a long time, the fight seethed on, each side declining to yield an inch of ground. Yet, eventually, it was Jean-Luc and Anaëlle's enduring purpose that conveyed the day. With a last push, they overpowered the French powers, driving them back into the valley underneath.

Triumph, in any case, included some significant downfalls. A considerable lot of their confidants lay fallen on the front line, their penance a demonstration of the cost of opportunity. Yet, in the savagery, there was trust — a gleam of light not too far off.

As the sun set over the mountains, projecting a brilliant tint across the scene, Jean-Luc and Anaëlle remained on an edge, reviewing the scene beneath. Somewhere far off, the French armed forces withdrew in confusion, their flags worn out and their spirits broken.

"We did it, Anaëlle," Jean-Luc murmured, his voice loaded up with feeling. "We won."

Anaëlle grinned, tears flickering in her eyes. "Indeed, Jean-Luc," she answered, her voice gagged proudly. "We won."

What's more, as they embraced underneath the blurring light of day, their hearts expanded with the information that they had accomplished the unthinkable — that they had manufactured a future worth battling for.

In the years that followed, Commander Jean-Luc and Anaëlle Moreau became legends of the Provence mountains, their names murmured in quiet tones by the people who recalled their boldness. Furthermore, however, the scars of war stayed carved upon their spirits, they found comfort in one another's arms, knowing that together, they had conquered each deterrent in their way.

Echoes of Revolution

In the clamoring heart of Paris, where cobblestone roads reverberated with the intense strides of visionaries and revolutionaries the same, Pierre Deschamps stepped with reason. His look burning with the fire of upset, he longed for a world liberated by the chains of mistreatment, where the standards of freedom, equity, and society weren't simple ways of talking but the actual substance of presence.

As Pierre explored the complex rear entryways, murmurs of dispute moved in the air, blending with the fragrance of newly prepared bread and the far-off thunder of discontent. It was a period of commotion when each corner held the commitment of resistance and the danger of retaliation.

"Have you heard the most recent news, Pierre?" a voice called out from the shadows, bringing him into a stealthy discussion.

"What news, Henri?" Pierre answered, his interest aroused as he inclined in nearer, his heart beating with expectation.

"They say Madame Laurent has energized one more gathering of opposition warriors," Henri murmured, his eyes glimmering with profound respect for the bold widow who thought for even a second to challenge oppression.

"Madame Laurent?" Pierre shouted, a flood of trust flowing through his veins. "She's an awe-inspiring phenomenon, that one. With her next to us, we may very well have a potential for success against the oppressors."

With restored assurance, Pierre proceeded with his excursion through the roads of Paris, his psyche burning with dreams of a more promising time to come. However, even as he pushed forward, the shadows of peril hid everywhere, taking steps to snuff out the fire of upset before it could light.

In the meantime, in the faintly lit corners of the city, Madame Laurent plotted her best course of action, her eyes blazing with rebellion as she tended to her kindred obstruction warriors.

"My companions," she started, her voice ringing out like a clarion call, "we stand on the incline of history. The opportunity has arrived to ascend and hold onto our fate, to push off the shackles of oppression and usher in another time of opportunity and equity."

Her words touched off a flash of resistance in the hearts of her confidants, filling them with a feeling of direction that rose above dread.

Together, they would oppose the could of the oppressors, furnished with only their fortitude and conviction.

However, as the obstruction accumulated strength, so too did their foes. Controller Dupont, a persevering master of the law, sneaked the roads with a resolute assurance, his steely look fixed on uncovering questions any place it might prowl.

"We should be careful," Madame Laurent cautioned, her voice low and dire. "The powers of response will remain determined to pulverize us. We should remain one stride ahead on the off chance that we are to arise triumphant."

Her words were a sobering sign of the dangerous way they strolled, yet even despite the difficulty, the purpose of the opposition stayed unshaken.

During the confusion and vulnerability, one figure arose as an encouraging sign for the discouraged masses: General Lafayette, a legend of the American Unrest, whose name reverberated through the roads like an energizing cry.

"General Lafayette has vowed his help to our goal," Pierre shouted, his voice touched with wonderment and profound respect. "With him driving the charge, we can't fall flat."

Thus, with General Lafayette next to them, the progressives walked forward, their strides repeating the heartbeat of a country near the very edge of change. It was a fight for the spirit of France, a battle between the powers of freedom and oppression, where each man and lady should pick where their faithfulness lies.

Eventually, it was a battle for opportunity, however a demonstration of the dauntless soul of mankind itself. Through penance and tirelessness, Pierre and his confidants manufactured a way towards a more promising time to come, where the standards of freedom, balance, and club would as of now not be only a fantasy, but a reality for a long time into the future.

The sun rose over Paris, giving occasion to feel qualms about its brilliant light on the city roads as Pierre and Henri met again, their countenances drawn with the heaviness of their common battle.

"Did you hear?" Henri asked, his voice scarcely over a murmur. "The ruler has dispatched more soldiers to control the agitation."

Pierre gripped his clenched hands, his jaw fixing earnestly. "Then we should try harder. We can't permit dread to direct our activities."

Henri gestured gravely, his eyes mirroring the glimmering fire of insubordination that consumed them. "We stand on the right half of history, old buddy. No measure of abuse can stifle the fire of insurgency."

Together, they cleared their path through the clamoring roads, where the air snapped with expectation and vulnerability. Each face they passed bore the sign of battle, the engraving of a general public near the very edge of progress.

As they moved toward the secret gathering place, a feeling of brotherhood wrapped them, a common bond manufactured in the pot of obstruction. Madame Laurent remained in the middle, her presence deserving admiration and appreciation from all who accumulated around her.

"My companions," she started, her voice consistent and relentless, "the opportunity has arrived to stand firm against oppression. We can't vacillate in that frame of mind of difficulty, for we convey inside us the deepest desires of ages yet unborn."

The group mumbled in understanding, their voices ascending in a tune of assurance. Everyone drag the scars of mistreatment, the injuries caused by a framework that looked to squash their soul.

Yet, at that time, they were not just people but rather an aggregate power for change, joined as they continued looking for a superior tomorrow. With each step they took, they walked nearer to their fate, where the commitment of opportunity looked for them on the opposite side.

Also, as the sun set over Paris, creating long shaded areas upon the city roads, Pierre and his friends stood tall notwithstanding difficulty, their purpose whole, their spirits steadfast. For in their souls consumed the fire of transformation, an encouraging sign that would direct them through the haziest of times.

Together, they would revise the course of history, not as vanquishers or rulers, but rather as heroes of freedom, correspondence, and society. Also, however, the street ahead would be loaded with risk and vulnerability, they wouldn't falter in that frame of mind to the reason.

For they were the vanguard of progress, the gatekeepers of a future at this point unwritten. What's more, the length of their souls beat with the musicality of unrest, they could never give up, never retreat. For theirs was a battle for themselves, however for all who hoped for an existence where opportunity ruled.

As Pierre and Henri navigated the clamoring roads of Paris, their discussion hummed with criticalness and assurance. The sun plunged underneath the skyline, creating long shaded areas upon the cobblestone ways, however their purpose stayed steadfast.

"The lord's soldiers will not scare us," Pierre pronounced, his voice reverberating against the old walls of the city. "We've confronted affliction previously, and we'll confront it once more. Our objective is simply, and we'll battle until the final gasp leaves our bodies."

Henri gestured in understanding, his eyes blazing with a savage assurance. "Without a doubt, old buddy. We can't permit dread to incapacitate us. Now is the ideal time to show the oppressors that we will not be cowed into accommodation."

Their strides enlivened as they moved toward the meeting point, where Madame Laurent looked for them with a steely determination. The flashing light of the lights cast spooky shadows across her face, yet her eyes ignited with an intense assurance.

"We've gotten word that the lord's powers are shutting in," Madame Laurent reported, her voice slicing through the strained environment. "Be that as it may, we won't yield. We will stand firm even with oppression and mistreatment."

The accumulated opposition warriors mumbled their arrangement, their spirits unflinching by the approaching danger of savagery. Everyone knew the dangers they confronted, yet they were ready to forfeit everything for the purpose they put stock in.

As night dropped upon the city, the air popped with strain, yet in the dimness, a flash of trust touched off in the hearts of the progressives. They were troopers in a battle for the spirit of their country, and they wouldn't rest until triumph was theirs.

The next days were laden with risk and vulnerability as the ruler's powers fixed their hold on the city. Yet, the obstruction contenders stayed immovable, their purpose whole by the approaching danger of brutality.

In the shadows of rear entryways and secret gathering places, they kept on plotting their best course of action, their spirits fearless by the always present risk that prowled everywhere.

"We can't permit ourselves to be threatened," Pierre announced, his voice ringing out with disobedience. "We should keep on battling for what we have confidence in, regardless of the expense."

His words reverberated with his friends, filling them with a reestablished feeling of direction and assurance. They realized that the street ahead would be troublesome, yet they were ready to confront anything challenges that came their direction.

Thus, they proceeded, their strides reverberating against the cobblestone roads as they walked nearer and nearer to their inescapable confrontation with the powers of mistreatment.

The unease in the air was overwhelming as the moment of retribution moved close. However, in the trepidation and vulnerability, there was likewise a feeling of calm assurance, a conviction that regardless of the situation, they were on the right half of history.

Also, when the last conflict came, they figured out it, and their hearts loaded up with mental fortitude and conviction. They battled for themselves, yet for people in the future who had the right to live in a world liberated from oppression and persecution.

Eventually, their penances were not to no end. However, many lives were lost in the battle, and their heritage lived on in the hearts and brains of the people who came after them.

For they were the legends of a transformation, the courageous people who thought for even a second to battle back for what they trusted in. What's more, however, their names might have been forgotten by history, but their soul persevered, an encouraging sign for all who hoped for a superior world.

Shadows of Intrigue

In the twisted roads of Paris, where the cobblestones reverberated with murmurs of interest and shadows whirled like phantoms, Joseph Fouquet moved with the covertness of a hunter. His presence was a demonstration of his dominance over the city's underside, a domain where power moved like sand in the breeze.

"One more evening, another game," Joseph mumbled to himself, his words lost during the chaos of the clamoring roads.

Marguerite Duval, his sidekick, skimmed close to him like a shadow. Her charm was as risky as a snake's kiss, all her developments a determined move toward their lethal dance. "Furthermore, what a game it will be, my dear Joseph," she murmured her voice a velvet touch that creeped him out.

Their organization was a sensitive harmony among trust and disloyalty, a tightrope strolls over an ocean of misdirection. In any case, as they explored the deceptive waters of Parisian culture, they realized their bond ran further than simple faithfulness; it was manufactured in the flames of aspiration and want.

In the meantime, Overseer Dupuis, a stronghold of equity in a city tormented by obscurity, chased them with an enthusiasm verging on fixation. His strides resonated like a roar in the thin rear entryways, his eyes burning with honorable fierceness.

"I'll get you, Fouquet! Regardless of the number of shadows you that conceal in, regardless of the number of networks you that twist," Dupuis promised, his assurance enduring.

Yet, in the disarray of their wait-and-see game, there was one soul trapped in the crossfire: Madame Claudette, a pawn in Joseph's hazardous game. Her destiny remained in a precarious situation, her supplications for benevolence overwhelmed by the commotion of the roads.

"Kindly, let me go," she argued, her voice shuddering with dread as Joseph's frosty look overwhelmed her. Be that as it may, he only laughed, his grin as cold as the cutting-edge he employed.

"Not yet, my dear Madame," he answered, his words dribbling with vindictiveness. "There are still moves to be made, pieces to be played. Furthermore, you, my dear, are the most important piece of all."

As strains mounted, Joseph and Marguerite wound up captured in their snare of duplicity, everything they might do examined by both companion and enemy. With Dupuis shutting in from all sides, they realized their there was no time left, that soon they would confront the outcomes of their activities.

In any case, even despite approaching destruction, Joseph and Marguerite wouldn't give up. They were survivors, warriors in this present reality where just the cleverness and the savage won.

"Eventually, it will be a skirmish of brains," Marguerite pronounced, her eyes blazing sincerely. "What's more, we will arise triumphant, regardless of the expense."

Thus, as the midnight hour drew nearer and Paris fell into a quieted tranquility, Joseph and Marguerite arranged for their last retribution. In a city where shadows murmured mysteries and each corner held another risk, simply the most grounded would get by, and just the cleverness would guarantee triumph.

Their means reverberated through the abandoned back streets, their breath blending with the delicate murmur of the night breeze. The air was weighty with expectation, every second pregnant with the chance of double-crossing or reclamation.

"At any point do you wonder, Joseph, on the off chance that it's all worth the effort?" Marguerite's voice sliced through the quiet like a blade, her words weighty with the heaviness of their wrongdoings.

Joseph stopped, his look waiting on the far-off shine of the city lights. "Some of the time," he conceded, his voice touched with lament. "However, what decision do we have? In a world controlled by power and ravenousness, we either play the game or become its casualties."

Marguerite gestured, her eyes mirroring the heap of shades of obscurity that prowled inside her spirit. "Sufficiently genuine," she yielded. "However, I can't resist the urge to contemplate whether there's something else to life besides this unending pattern of duplicity and selling out."

Their discussion was interfered with by the unexpected appearance of a figure rising out of the shadows, his outline framed against the weak gleam of the moon. It was Overseer Dupuis, his look penetrating as he stared at Joseph.

"I've at last found you, Fouquet," Dupuis pronounced, his voice a low snarl that resonated during that time air. "Your rule of fear closes this evening."

Joseph's lips twisted into a sneer, his certainty enduring despite looming destruction. "Is that thus, Examiner?" he answered, his tone ridiculing. "I'm apprehensive you'll track down that I'm not effortlessly crushed."

With that, he changed direction suddenly and vanished into obscurity, Marguerite following not far behind like a faithful dog next to him. Dupuis watched them go; his clenched hands grasped in disappointment as he understood that the game was nowhere near finished.

As they cleared their path through the twisted roads of Paris, Joseph and Marguerite could feel the heaviness of Dupuis' interest pushing downward on them like a weighty shroud. Yet, they would not be dissuaded, their purpose resolute as they continued onward into the unexplored world.

"We can't continue to run perpetually, Joseph," Marguerite forewarned, her voice touched with desperation. "Sometime, Dupuis will find us, and afterward what?"

Joseph's jaw grasped, his psyche dashing with the potential outcomes that lay ahead. "Then, at that point, we'll deal with him directly," he announced, his voice firm. "We might be outlaws, yet we're not quitters. Whatever occurs, we'll confront it together."

Their process drove them to the edges of the city, where the roads gave approach to rambling fields washed in the delicate gleam of the moon. It was here that they made their stand, their options somewhat limited as they anticipated Dupuis' unavoidable appearance.

Furthermore, show up he did, his strides reverberating through the tranquility of the night like a harbinger of destruction. With a decided sparkle in his eye, he rose out of the shadows, his look locked on Joseph with unfaltering power.

"It's finished, Fouquet," Dupuis proclaimed, his voice ringing out like a shot in the quietness. "You're encircled, and there's no place left to run."

Joseph met his look with a steely determination, his jaw set in a resistant line. "Maybe," he yielded. "Yet, that doesn't mean we're going down easily."

With that, the two men thrusted at one another, their clenched hands crashing in a whirlwind of blows that reverberated as the night progressed. Marguerite was observed as a passive spectator, her heart beating in her chest as she petitioned God for their triumph.

The fight seethed on, each man battling with a fierceness brought into the world of franticness and assurance. It was a conflict of titans, a battle for incomparability that would decide the destiny of all.

Eventually, it was Joseph who became successful, his solidarity and shrewd demonstration a lot for Dupuis to survive. With a last, conclusive blow, he debilitated the investigator, leaving him to spread on the ground like a wrecked doll.

As Joseph stood victorious during the destruction of their fight, he couldn't resist the opportunity to feel an ache of regret for the man he had vanquished. Regardless of their disparities, Dupuis had been a commendable foe, an amazing powerhouse in reality as we know it where not many thoughts for even a moment to challenge him.

However, there was no time for wistfulness, not when their own lives remained in a critical state. With Marguerite next to him, Joseph vanished into the night again, abandoning the bedlam and slaughter of their showdown.

As they liquefied into the dimness, their future unsure and their past loaded up with second thoughts, Joseph and Marguerite realized that their process was not even close to finished. In any case, anything that preliminaries lay ahead, they would confront them together, limited by a bond that would never be broken.

Eventually, they were something beyond sidekicks; they were survivors, warriors in our current reality where just the craftiness and the merciless won. What's more, the same length as they had one another, they realized they could defeat anything that held them up.

Whispers of Betrayal

In the core of the French armed forces, in the bedlam of war, General Dupont remained as a transcending figure of power, his order resounding through the positions like a deafening drumbeat. His very presence bore the heaviness of endless fights, a demonstration of his unflinching devotion to Sovereign Napoleon and his tireless quest for triumph. However, behind the façade of emotionless assurance, snuck a whirlwind of aspiration and want, driving him at any point forward as he continued looking for power and magnificence.

Colonel Pierre, a confided-in friend to the general, watched with a combination of esteem and worry as Dupont's desires took off higher than ever. Pierre's dedication to his boss conflicted with his feeling of obligation to his nation, leaving him conflicted between his devotion and his still, small voice notwithstanding mounting injustice and interest.

In the tumult of the camp, Commander Charles arose as an honorable guide and mental fortitude, an unflinching safeguard of the country's respectability. His immovable commitment enlivened his friends to stand firm against the infringing shadows of disloyalty, their determination enduring even in the haziest of hours.

Discussions hummed through the camp like a hive of honey bees, blending with the rattle of arms and the drifter of boots. Warriors discussed the dependability of their chiefs, their voices ascending in enlivened conversation as coalitions moved like sand in the breeze.

"Have you seen the overall's most recent moves?" one warrior questioned, his temple wrinkled with concern. "It likens to desire if you were to ask me."

"Ok, yet desire drives significance," one more countered, a glimmer of reverence in his eyes. "General Dupont looks for just to get the eventual fate of our country."

Pierre tuned in peacefully, his psyche whirling with clashing feelings. He figured out the risk of visually impaired faithfulness, yet he was unable to force himself to leave the man he had followed into incalculable fights.

In the interim, General Dupont's plans developed perpetually daring, his eyes fixed solidly on the high position that appeared to be barely too far. He murmured commitments of greatness to the people who might follow him, turning a snare of misleading that took steps to trap the whole armed force in its tangled hug.

Be that as it may, Chief Charles stayed unfaltering in his standards, his steady devotion a brilliant illustration to all who considered remaining against the tide of defilement. He revitalized his companions with expressions of mental fortitude and conviction, his voice a clarion call in the bedlam of war.

"Stand firm, my companions," he encouraged, his look immovable. "For we battle for ourselves, however for the fate of our country. Allow distinction to be our aide, and triumph will be our own."

The conflict of arms reverberated across the front line, the air thick with the harsh aroma of explosives and the calls of the injured. General Dupont's powers flooded forward with a savagery brought into the world of urgency, their chief's desires driving them ever forward.

In any case, Pierre could never again disregard the reality that lay before him. As he watched his companions fall during the most intense part of the conflict, he realized that he could never again sit around and permit Dupont's unfairness to carry on without some kind of imposed limit.

"That's it," he proclaimed, his voice slicing through the mayhem like a sharp edge through silk. "We should stop this franticness before it consumes every one of us."

With crushing sadness, Pierre betrayed his previous commandant, his faithfulness currently committed to a more noble end goal. Along with Chief Charles and the people who stayed consistent with the praiseworthy standards and honesty, he battled to stem the tide of debasement that took steps to immerse their dearest country.

The fight seethed on, every second full of risk and vulnerability. Yet, eventually, it was not the cold of arms or the fuss of war that decided the destiny of France, but the unfaltering determination of the people who would not respect the obscurity that snuck inside the hearts of men.

As the residue settled and the air cleared, General Dupont remained solitary, his fantasies of force and magnificence broken by the inflexible walk of equity. In his loss, he filled in as an obvious suggestion to all who might allow desire to daze them to the genuine importance of honor and dependability.

What's more, however, the scars of war would wait long in the recollections of the people who had battled and drained upon the war zone, they would likewise act as a demonstration of the dauntless soul of humankind, and the force of fortitude and conviction to conquer even the best of preliminaries.

The Rose of Versailles

In the brilliant corridors of Versailles, where the air was thick with interest and murmurs of embarrassment, Juliette Dubois skimmed like a dream of elegance and excellence. All Her means directed consideration, her presence a demonstration of the refinement of her childhood. As the girl of a well-off blue-blood, she was no more peculiar to the extravagances and excess that encompassed her.

Yet, past the veneer of riches and honor, Juliette held onto confidentiality, a longing that beat underneath her made outside. It was a longing for something more significant than the sparkling knickknacks of court life — a longing for affection.

What's more, the love she saw was in the most surprising of spots, in the arms of Pierre Rousseau, a capable craftsman whose deep look punctured through her protections. Their adoration was a fire that glimmered disobediently against the chill of cultural assumptions, rising above the limits of class and station.

However, similar to a shadow prowling in the murkiness, Count Henri cast his greedy look upon Juliette. With his haughty disposition and tremendous riches, he viewed her as just an award to be won, a prize to enhance his arm.

Pierre, nonetheless, saw Juliette as far beyond a simple victory. As far as he might be concerned, she was the dream who lighted his enthusiasm, the motivation behind each stroke of his brush. Theirs was an affection brought into the world of close companions, an affection that had no limits.

In any case, as the pressure between Pierre and Count Henri arrived at a crescendo, Juliette ended up conflicted between obligation and want. Trapped in the crossfire of their contention, she attempted to accommodate her heart's yearning with the assumptions set upon her.

It was in these wild times that Juliette tracked down comfort in the insight of Madame Celeste, her mom and partner. With a delicacy brought into the world of a mother's affection, Madame Celeste urged Juliette to follow the directs of her heart, to seek after the way that would prompt genuine joy.

Thus, with fortitude beating through her veins, Juliette pursued her decision. She would challenge the shows of society, neglecting the solaces of her special childhood for the commitment of an affection that consumed her more brilliantly than any star in the night sky.

As she remained before Pierre, her hand caught in his, Juliette realized that she had pursued the ideal choice. For at that time, she was not simply Juliette Dubois, a little girl of a blue-blood — she was Juliette, the modeler of her predetermination, the escort of her own heart.

What's more, however, the street ahead would be full of difficulties and impediments, Juliette confronted the future with a recently discovered feeling of direction and assurance. For she knew that as long as she had Pierre close by, she could endure any hardship that came her direction.

Thus, as the sun plunged underneath the skyline and the stars started to sparkle in the velvet sky, Juliette and Pierre set out on their excursion together, their adoration enlightening the murkiness like an encouraging sign for all who hoped for an affection that exceeded all rational limitations.

Their romantic tale murmured through the hallways of Versailles, turned into a discussion of the court. Tattles swayed their tongues, scandalized by the boldness of Juliette's disobedience, yet furtively jealous of the enthusiasm that consumed her and Pierre.

In the rich loftiness of the royal residence, Juliette and Pierre found snapshots of taken ecstasy, taken away to segregated gardens and secret recesses where they could be distant from everyone else together. In those taken minutes, time appeared to stop, the rest of the world blurring into irrelevance as they lost themselves in one another's hug.

However, their satisfaction was not to endure. Count Henri, his pride injured by Juliette's dismissal, promised to destroy them no holds barred. He conspired and plotted, winding around a trap of untruths and misdirection intended to split apart Juliette and Pierre.

From the outset, Juliette wouldn't completely accept the tales that flowed about Pierre, sticking to the conviction that their affection was sufficiently able to endure any test. In any case, as the proof mounted and questions crawled into her heart, she wound up conflicted between devotion to Pierre and the need to safeguard her standing.

In her haziest minutes, Juliette went to Madame Celeste for direction, looking for the insight of a consistently positioned girl's mother's satisfaction regardless of anything else. With tears in her eyes, she admitted her feelings of dread and questions, her voice shuddering with vulnerability.

However, Madame Celeste's reaction was unflinching in its conviction. "Depend on your instinct, my dear," she guided, her voice delicate yet firm. "Genuine affection merits battling for, regardless of the expense."

Encouraged by her mom's words, Juliette made plans to stand up to Pierre and request reality. With crushing sadness, she searched him out, her means floundering as she prepared herself for what she could find.

At the point when she found him, alone in his studio, his face pale and drawn with stress, Juliette realized that the snapshot of retribution had come. With shaking hands, she faced him, her voice stifled with feeling as she uncovered her apprehensions and doubts.

From the start, Pierre denied everything, his protestations ringing empty in Juliette's ears. Yet, as she squeezed him for replies, his façade disintegrated, and he admitted reality — the reality of his past, of the obligations he owed and the untruths he had told to safeguard her.

At that time, Juliette's reality broke. The man she cherished, the man she had endowed with her heart, remained before her a more interesting, his double-crossing cutting further than any sharp edge. Misery tore through her like a typhoon, leaving her heaving for breath as she battled to get a handle on the destruction of her fantasies.

In any case, even at her breaking point, Juliette tracked down a glint of trust — a flicker of the strength and versatility that had consistently characterized her. With a steely determination, she confronted Pierre one last time, her voice cold and steady as she conveyed her decision.

"It's finished," she murmured, her words reverberating in the quiet of the room. "I can't pardon you for what you've done."

Also, with that, she dismissed and strolled, her heart weighty with distress but her soul whole. Juliette realizes that even in the profundities of sadness, she would track down the solidarity to rise once more, to reconstruct her life from the remains of her broken dreams.

In the days that followed, Juliette withdrew from the court, looking for comfort in the hug of her family and the solace of natural environmental factors. Gradually, the injuries started to recuperate, the aggravation of Pierre's double-crossing giving way to a feeling of calm renunciation.

However, she attempted to cover the memory of their adoration underneath a facade of lack of concern, Juliette would never fully shake the phantom of Pierre's touch — the memory of his lips against hers, his arms around her, holding her nearby.

Thus, as the years passed and the reverberations of their adoration blurred into the far-off past, Juliette conveyed with her a piece of Pierre's heart — a piece that would continuously have a place with her, regardless of where life's process could lead.

Eventually, Juliette realized that affection was not only a transitory enthusiasm or a fleeting interest — it was a power as immortal and persevering as the actual stars, a power that would direct her on her excursion, any place it could take her.

The Enigma of Elba

The island of Elba, covered in fog and secret, remained as a singular sentinel in the tremendous region of the Mediterranean Ocean. Its rough shores demonstrated the veracity of the rhythmic movement of history, a quiet observer of the ascent and fall of realms. Among its rough bluffs and secret bays, a show unfurled that would reverberate through the chronicles of time.

Skipper Louis, a man of steadfast faithfulness and steely purpose, watched the shoreline with the persistence of a vigilant watchman. Each step he took resounded with the heaviness of obligation, an indication of his unbreakable commitment to safeguard his country no matter what. The cadenced run of waves into the shore gave a background to his viewpoints as he checked the skyline, his eyes sharp and careful.

"One more day, another watch," Louis murmured to himself, changing the edge of his tricorn cap against the pungent breeze. The tang of salt blended with the fragrance of ocean splash, filling his lungs with the inebriating smell of the sea. He strolled with reason, his strides reverberating against the stones like a consistent drumbeat.

As he watched the shoreline, Louis couldn't shake the sensation of disquiet that waited in the air like a thick mist. The island appeared to pause its breathing, as though sitting tight for something earth-shattering to happen. Much to his dismay just into the great beyond, the wheels of fate were at that point moving.

In the meantime, in the core of the island, Maria Bonaparte moved with an effortlessness and class befitting her illustrious genealogy. Her steady faithfulness to her sibling, Napoleon, was the stuff of legends, an encouraging sign in the haziest of times. She gave solace and backing to Napoleon in his exile, her presence a wellspring of solidarity in the tempest of vulnerability.

"Sibling," she murmured, her voice delicate and relieving. "Try not to lose trust. We will figure out how to beat this."

Napoleon, when the expert of Europe, presently ended up restricted to the shores of Elba, his fantasies of success decreased to simple murmurs on the breeze. However, even in bondage, his soul stayed whole, a fire that would not be quenched.

"Maria," he answered, his voice loaded up sincerely. "I might be detained; however, my soul is sans still. They can't chain me until the end of time."

Across the island, Colonel Bertrand moved with the covertness of a hunter, his psyche a hurricane of plans and tricks. A believed compatriot of Napoleon, he plotted to help his ruler break from Elba, all his moves a determined ruse in the round of force and legislative issues.

"Lead representative Montrose might think himself smart," Bertrand pondered, his lips twisting into a guileful grin. "Be that as it may, he underrates the purpose of a Bonaparte."

Lead representative Montrose, a harsh and inflexible figure of English power, watched over the island with a vigilant eye. His orders were clear: Napoleon should be kept restricted, and his impact contained no matter what.

"I won't permit Elba to turn into a favorable place for defiance," Montrose pronounced, his voice unfaltering. "The ruler will remain our detainee, regardless."

Trapped in the crossfire of dependability and obligation was Lieutenant Pierre, a youthful trooper conflicted between his faithfulness to his nation and his reverence for Napoleon. His heart throbbed with the heaviness of his clashing loyalties, his brain a praiseworthy milestone and obligation.

"What decision do I have?" Pierre pondered so anyone might hear, his voice touched with dissatisfaction. "To deceive my head or my country? Is there no center ground?"

As strains stewed and the apparition of defiance lingered ever bigger, the destiny of Elba remained in a precarious situation. It was a fight for opportunity, yet for the actual soul of a country, where the lines between good and bad are obscured as time passes.

Eventually, it was not swords or guns that determined the destiny of Elba, but the boldness and assurance of the people who thought for even a second to challenge the chains of mistreatment. Napoleon and his supporters ascended against their detainers; their voices brought up in a resistant chorale of freedom.

"Vive l'Empereur!" they cried, their words a mobilizing weep for all who yearned for opportunity.

Furthermore, however, their battle was long and full of danger, they arose triumphant eventually, their penance a demonstration of the getting force of the human soul. For on the distant island of Elba, where the waves murmured privileged insights and the breeze conveyed reverberations of unrest, history was made and legends were conceived.

Echoes of Waterloo

In the wild mayhem of the combat zone, Sergeant Jacques ended up dug in a terrible battle for endurance upon the blood-doused fields of Waterloo. The bitter fragrance of smoke filled his nose, blending with the metallic tang of blood, as he battled with all the intensity his fatigued body could marshal. Each swing of his edge was met with a reverberating conflict as it slammed into foe steel, the clamor of fight overwhelming any remaining sound put something aside for the calls of the injured and the deafening thunder of gun shoot.

Alongside him, his confidants battled with equivalent boldness, their countenances set in horrid assurance as they clung tightly against the tireless development of the adversary. Through the murkiness of smoke and residue, Jacques saw Lieutenant Pierre, his appearance one of steely purpose in the bedlam.

"Sergeant!" Pierre's voice sliced through the racket, his eyes blazing with criticalness. "We should hold this line! For France!"

Jacques gestured; his jaw set in a firm line as he repeated the lieutenant's feeling. "For France," he answered, his voice scarcely discernible over the tumult as he arranged to figure out the foe.

The lieutenant's look cleared across the front line, his brain dashing to form a technique during the turmoil of the fight. "We want fortifications on the eastern flank," he yelled over the uproar. "Sergeant, accumulate a crew and stand firm on that footing no matter what!"

With a quick gesture, Jacques gathered a gathering of men, their countenances carved with assurance despite the exhaustion that weighed vigorously upon them. "You heard the lieutenant," he howled over the thunder of fight. "We hold this ground!"

As they moved to build up the eastern flank, the voice of Colonel Dupont rang out like a clarion call, imparting a restored feeling of assurance in the hearts of his men. "Stand firm, men!" he cried, his words an encouraging sign in the bedlam. "For ruler and country!"

The men around Jacques cheered, their spirits floated by the colonel's enduring determination. With restored assurance, they prepared themselves against the foe's tireless attack, their swords blazing in the daylight as they battled with each ounce of solidarity they had.

Yet, even as they battled with bravery and assurance, they realized that triumph was nowhere near guaranteed. Across the field,

General Wellington drove his powers with a steely assurance, everything he might do determined to achieve the destruction of Napoleon's military.

"We should break their lines!" Marshal Ney's deafening voice resonated across the war zone as he drove a considering charge against the English powers. His men followed him with resolute steadfastness, their swords glimmering in the daylight as they charged head-first into the fight.

However, despite their savage endeavors, the result of the fight stayed questionable. It was a battle that rose above simple engagement, a conflict of philosophies and desires where each individual had to face their loyalties and convictions.

As the fight seethed on, Sergeant Jacques and his friends battled with a mental fortitude brought into the world of urgency, each blow struck a demonstration of their unflinching assurance to protect their country from the people who tried to oppress it. Furthermore, however, the chances appeared to be unfavorable, they wouldn't yield, their spirits whole in that frame of mind of affliction.

"We won't vacillate!" Jacques' voice transcended the bedlam of the fight, his words a mobilizing sob for people around him. "For France and opportunity!"

With those words reverberating in their souls, they proceeded, their purpose relentless even as the fight seethed on around them. For on the blood-splashed fields of Waterloo, during the stunning conflict of steel and the booming thunder of gun discharge, they realize that their penance would be associated with ages to come — a demonstration of the unstoppable soul of mankind notwithstanding overpowering chances.

However, during the turmoil of the fight, there were snapshots of passing clearness, where the confusion of mass conflict lifted for the briefest of minutes, uncovering the distinct truth. Also, in those minutes, Sergeant Jacques ended up wrestling with the hugeness of the undertaking before him, the heaviness of obligation resting vigorously upon his shoulders.

As he studied the combat zone, his eyes cleared over the endless fallen, their inert structures a terrible sign of the expense of war. Every life lost was a misfortune, a spirit doused chasing magnificence and honor. But, in the gloom, there was a flash of trust — a glint of plausibility that energized Jacques' determination to proceed, to battle for a future where such forfeits wouldn't be to no end.

As time passed, the commotion of the fight developed stronger, the conflict of steel and the thunder of cannon fire reverberating across the blood-splashed fields like an orchestra of obliteration. But, during the confusion, there was an unusual feeling of brotherhood — a bond produced in the cauldron of war that rose above rank and station.

Next to Jacques, Confidential Leclerc battled with a fierceness that misrepresented his childhood, all his developments a demonstration of his assurance to show what he can do in the war zone. "Cling tightly, Sergeant!" he yelled over the commotion, his voice touched with a blend of dread and fervor. "We won't be crushed!"

Jacques gestured, a terrible grin playing at the edges of his lips as he traded a knowing look with the youthful trooper. "We stand together, Private," he answered, his voice consistent despite the bedlam that encompassed them. "For France."

Thus, they battled on, their sharp edges blazing in the daylight as they conflicted with the foe over and over. As time passed, the tide of the fight moved, the benefit swinging ever-changing like a pendulum as the two militaries conflicted in a frantic battle for matchless quality.

Be that as it may, in the disarray and butchery, there were snapshots of surprising excellence — a brief look at humankind in the mercilessness of war. As the sun plunged underneath the skyline, projecting a warm sparkle across the war zone, Sergeant Jacques ended up quickly mesmerized by seeing a solitary blossom, its fragile petals spreading out during the destruction.

Briefly, the repulsions of war blurred out of the spotlight, supplanted by a feeling of stunningness and marvel at the versatility of life in the bedlam. Furthermore, at that time, Jacques felt a reestablished feeling of direction — an assurance to battle for triumph, yet for the commitment of a superior tomorrow.

As the fight seethed on into the evening, the calls of the injured and the withering reverberated across the blood-doused fields, an eerie indication of the expense of war. But, during the depression, there was a promising sign — a glimmer of light that would not be stifled.

For on the blood-drenched fields of Waterloo, during the conflict of steel and the thunder of gun discharge, Sergeant Jacques and his confidants battled for triumph, yet for the beliefs and rules that they held dear. Furthermore, however, the result of the fight stayed unsure, one thing was clear — their penance would reverberate through the records of history, a demonstration of the getting force of the human soul notwithstanding overpowering chances.

The Phoenix of St. Helena

On the far-off island of St. Helena, a spot known for its devastation and unforgiving scene, a far-fetched adventure unfurled, opposing the imperatives of existence. Here, during the crashing waves and rough shores, Napoleon Bonaparte, the once-strong ruler of France, ended up banished and broken, his fantasies of success diminished to simple murmurs in the breeze.

Longwood House, the home where Napoleon lived, remained as an image of his bondage, walls demonstrating the veracity of the wild feelings stirred inside. However, in the misery, there was one enduring presence that offered comfort to the fallen ruler - Madame Marie.

With her enduring reliability and delicate disposition, Madame Marie became Napoleon's worker, however his friend, a guide of light in his haziest hours. Their discussions reverberated through the lobbies, as Napoleon thought back about the times of his victories, his voice touched with wistfulness.

"Madame Marie, do you recall the days when the world shuddered at my name?" Napoleon would muse, his look fixed on the far-off skyline.

"Indeed, Your Highness," Madame Marie would answer, her voice a mitigating tune. "Yet, significance is estimated by triumphs, yet in addition by the hearts you contacted en route."

In the meantime, lead representative Reynolds, the English authority entrusted with managing Napoleon's exile, watched with a blend of fear and scorn as the fallen sovereign's impact kept on waiting on the island.

"We can't permit him to recapture his power," Reynolds proclaimed harshly to his counselors, his voice resonating through the corridors of force. "We should fix our grasp on him no matter what."

However, notwithstanding Reynolds' earnest attempts to keep up with control, there was a developing feeling of turmoil among the occupants of St. Helena. Murmurs of disobedience drifted through the air like a taboo mystery, as supporters and supporters unobtrusively plotted to liberate their cherished head from imprisonment.

Among these plotters was Chief Henri, a youthful official conflicted between his obligation to his nation and his relentless devotion to Napoleon. With a feeling of obligation that consumed more brilliance than any fire, he promised to support the ruler's getaway, regardless of the results.

"Skipper Henri, are you sure about this strategy?" an individual official addressed, his voice bound with concern. "You risk everything for an at this point not in manpower."

Henri fixed his friend with a steely look. "He may never again wear the crown, yet he is as yet our sovereign," he answered, his voice fearless. "Furthermore, I won't sit around while he experiences someplace far off, banished in shame."

As pressures mounted among Napoleon and his detainers, the island of St. Helena turned into a dangerous situation prepared to detonate all of a sudden. Each murmured discussion, each stealthy look, was a demonstration of the stewing discontent that took steps to bubble over into open defiance.

Yet, during the confusion and vulnerability, there was a good omen - the unfaltering assurance of the people who would not acknowledge the rout. As time passed, Napoleon and his followers arranged for the unavoidable confrontation with their oppressors, their purpose unshakeable notwithstanding misfortune.

Thus, on a game-changing day that would be scratched into the records of history, the island of St. Helena turned into a landmark for opportunity, as the powers of oppression conflicted with the people who thought for even a moment to oppose them.

The sound of gunfire reverberated through the air, blending with the calls of the mistreated and the yells of the resistant. It was an endurance battle, a battle for the spirit of a country, where each man and lady should pick where their loyalties lie.

Eventually, it was a fight for opportunity, yet a demonstration of the persevering force of the human soul - an update that even in the most obscure of times, trust can in any case thrive, and dreams can, in any case, take off. What's more, however, Napoleon might have been crushed in the fight, his heritage would live on in the hearts of the people who hoped for a superior world.

Epilogue:

As the sun plunged underneath the skyline, projecting its brilliant tones across the sky, it checked the finish of one more day, however the finish of an epochal period - the Napoleonic time. Afterward, the world stood changed, always formed by the wild situation that had transpired throughout the previous many years. Wars had been pursued, upsets had cleared across landmasses, and domains had risen and fallen like the tides of history.

However, during the confusion and commotion, there existed a significant feeling of coherence, a string that bound together the past, present, and future. The reverberations of history resounded through the chronicles of time, their reverberation felt in the hearts and brains of ages to come. From the terrific lobbies of capacity to the humblest of towns, the examples learned and the tales told during this period would persevere, their effect enduring a long way past the limits of time.

As a result of war and unrest, the world arose perpetually different, its predetermination unavoidably modified by the activities of the people who hoped for a superior future. The old request had been broken, its leftovers cleared away by the tide of progress and change. In its place, new realms rose, their establishments

120

based upon the desires not entirely set in stone to fashion their fates.

However, during the recurring pattern of history, one thing stayed steady: the unyielding soul of mankind. Through the haziest days and the fiercest tempests, it persevered, tough and unfaltering even with affliction. However long there were hearts loaded up with boldness and psyches on fire with enthusiasm, the tradition of the Napoleonic period would live on, a demonstration of the getting through force of the human soul to defeat even the best of difficulties.

The narratives of this period, deified in the records of time, were filled in as a demonstration of the victories and hardships of the human experience. From the front lines of Waterloo to the salons of Paris, from the shores of St. Helena to the deserts of Focal Asia, they discussed boldness, penance, and the unwavering quest for opportunity and equity. In the existence of the people who thought about challenging shows and fashioned their predeterminations, we find reverberations of our battles and wins, tokens of the unstoppable soul that exists in all of us.

Thus, as we bid goodbye to the Imperial Sagas, let us not grieve the death of a period, yet praise the getting through the tradition of the people who hoped against hope and thought for even a moment to act. For in their accounts, we track down motivation and trust, a directing light to enlighten the way ahead in a world consumed by confusion and vulnerability. As we turn the last page of this part ever, let us convey forward the illustrations learned and the recollections appreciated, for they are the genuine fortunes of the human experience, and they will persevere for a long time into the future.

Echoes from the Himalayas: Nabal's Literary Canvas

Setting out on the excursion of life in the curious town of Chhachar, Pithoragarh, India, on the third of July 1968, I, Nabal Kishore Pande, tracked down my underlying foundations in a humble family. Brought into the world to Mrs. Urmila Pandey and Mr. P C Pandey, my working-class childhood ingrained values that have formed my personality and uncommonly moved me.

From early on, I displayed an inborn interest, in exploring different avenues regarding the two words and my general surroundings. This intrinsic quality would later bloom into enthusiasm for narrating, making way for a special combination of specialized accuracy and endless inventiveness.

My scholastic process drove me down the way of electrical designing, a discipline that equipped me with specialized sharpness. Be that as it may, my heart tracked down comfort in the domain of words, where I could wind around stories and investigate the tremendous scope of the creative mind. This duality characterized my initial years, making me ready for an exceptional change from an electrical designer to a multi-layered person.

On the eleventh of May 2003, my life accepted one more huge turn as I entered the domain of marriage with Bhagwati Pandey. The following years delivered the happy event of becoming a pleased dad on the 28th of October 2005, with the appearance of our daughter, Mahak. Family, as far as I might be concerned, turned into the anchor in the ocean of life's undertakings.

Quick forward to the present, and I end up dwelling in the tranquil hug of the Himalayan unassuming community of Pithoragarh. This beautiful setting fills in as both a dream and scenery to my ongoing livelihood - a full-time creator.

A Literary Odyssey:
My introduction to the universe of fiction blossomed from a real love for narrating. Equipped with an electrical science certification, I flawlessly merged specialized accuracy with an unrestrained creative mind, bringing about the production of more than 35 distributed books crossing different classifications.

CryptoCanvas NFT Frontier: My scholarly material investigates the suggestive scenes of the "CryptoCanvas NFT Frontier." This work takes perusers on an excursion into the computerized domain, where craftsmanship and innovation merge, making an embroidery of remarkable encounters.

Ace Your ACT, Excel on the SAT: The essential bits of knowledge embodied in "Ace Your ACT, Excel on the SAT" mirror my obligation to instructive greatness. Overcoming any barrier between specialized ability and scholastic achievement, this book fills in as an aide for hopeful understudies exploring state-sanctioned tests.

Lethal Illusion I, Lethal Illusion II: Inside the pages of "Lethal Illusion I, Lethal Illusion II, and its continuation, I dig into the perplexing domains of secret and anticipation. These works exhibit my capacity to enrapture perusers with accounts that keep them as eager and anxious as ever.

Kaleidoscope of Emotions: "**Kaleidoscope of Emotions**" disentangles the complexities of the human mind, introducing a different assortment of stories that navigate the profound range. This treasury fills in as a demonstration of the profundity and broadness of my imaginative soul.

Tech Veil: Navigating Future Shadows: In "Tech Veil: Navigating Future Shadows," I investigate the crossing point of innovation and society. This interesting piece dives into the expected effects of future progressions, offering experiences in exploring the strange region of the mechanical scene.

Every one of these scholarly works remains a demonstration of the amicable mix of my specialized foundation and innovative soul. Through my words, I mean to overcome any barrier between the logical and the creative, welcoming perusers into a reality where different features of life flawlessly coincide.

Connecting with the World Through Words: My general objective is to lay out an association with the world through my scholarly undertakings. Words, as far as I might be concerned, are a method for correspondence as well as a door to shared encounters and feelings. In a world that is continually developing, I endeavor to make stories that reverberate with the human experience, rising above limits and cultivating understanding.

As I keep on exploring the unpredictable embroidered artwork of life in the hug of the Himalayas, I welcome perusers to go along with me on this excursion. Through the force of words, I try to make a permanent imprint on hearts and brains, making an enduring heritage that rises above the pages of my books.

In the modest community of Pithoragarh, amid the glorious Himalayas, the excursion from an electrical specialist to a creator has been a groundbreaking odyssey. It is a demonstration of the consistent combination of specialized accuracy and unfathomable imagination, an excursion that I am anxious to impart to the world.